ADVENTURES
IN A VIDEO GAME

DON'T CLIMB
THIS MOUNTAIN

OTHER BOOKS BY DUSTIN BRADY

ADVENTURES IN A VIDEO GAME

DON'T CLIMB THIS MOUNTAIN

DUSTIN BRADY

ART BY JESSE BRADY

Andrews McMeel
PUBLISHING®

Andrews McMeel Publishing
a division of Andrews McMeel Universal
1130 Walnut Street, Kansas City, Missouri 64106
www.andrewsmcmeel.com

Hacked font by David Libeau

24 25 26 27 28 SDB 10 9 8 7 6 5 4 3 2 1

ISBN Paperback: 978-1-5248-7707-1
ISBN Hardback: 978-1-5248-7942-6

Library of Congress Control Number: 2024933266

Made by:
RR Donnelley (Guangdong) Printing Solutions Company Ltd
Address and location of manufacturer:
No. 2, Minzhu Road, Daning, Humen Town,
Dongguan City, Guangdong Province, China 523930
1st Printing—5/20/24

CONTENTS

DEAR ADVENTURER,

Did you know that one dollar of lemons can produce nearly thirteen dollars of lemonade? That's what we call an inspiring statistic!

Several years ago, the Bionosoft Corporation trapped a bunch of kids inside of video games. That was a bummer. A true lemon of a story. Fortunately, the U.S. government stepped in to create lemonade out of that lemon—delicious, refreshing, expensive lemonade.

The brand-new Agency of Virtual Adventure Regulation, Inspection, and Compliance Enforcement (a.k.a. AVARICE) is dedicated to making Bionosoft "trapped in a video game" technology safe and fun for all. AVARICE is forming partnerships with entertainment brands worldwide to bring regular, everyday people like yourself into video games.

"Wait," you might be saying. "Isn't that dangerous?"
Don't be such a lemon.

To ensure that every adventure is as safe, fun, and profitable as possible, we at AVARICE have asked our partners to please not trap anyone inside of video games. Actually, our exact words were "pretty please," which is about as strong of a "please" as you can get. Also, it has recently come to our attention that Bionosoft technology may allow characters from video games to enter the real world and cause minor mayhem. To prevent this, we've asked our partners to "pretty please with sugar on top" not let that happen. We are proud to report that is the English language's strongest possible "please."

So pretty please with sugar on top, enjoy your adventure in a video game. Take comfort in the AVARICE motto: "Nothing could possibly go wrong now!"™

SINCERELY,
YOUR FRIENDS AT AVARICE

CHAPTER ONE

HYYYYPE!

"Three. Two. One. Go."

Archie smiled at the camera, took a deep breath, then started his video the same way his hero started every video: by screaming the word "hype" as long as his lungs would allow.

"Hyyyyyyyyyyyyyyyyyyype! What up, hypeheads, this is Archie Maroney, a.k.a. the Archmaster General, a.k.a. the Golden Arch, a.k.a. . . ."

"Stop, stop, stop," Archie's camerawoman said. "It's not recording."

Archie closed his eyes. "Is it because you forgot to hit record again?"

"Nope! Wait. OK, maybe. But I got it now!"

Archie kept his eyes closed for a few seconds longer and reminded himself that Mae was seven years old. When he became a famous YouTuber, he could afford to hire a professional, but until then, he'd have to be thankful for the free labor his little cousin provided as well as the complicated camera her dad let her borrow. "The light turns red when it's recording."

"That's how I knew it wasn't recording!" Mae replied.

"So don't say 'go' until you see the red light."

"Great tip, Arch! Three, two, one, go."

"Hyyyyyyyyyyyyy . . ."

"Stop, stop, stop. OK, now go."

Archie wondered what Sir Hype would do in this situation. He found himself wondering that often. When most people watched Sir Hype, they saw the Lamborghini. They saw the mansion with the waterslides and shark tank. They saw that video where he dives into a tower full of gold coins. When Archie watched Sir Hype, he saw inspiration. He saw a rags-to-riches story. He saw Roy Ferguson.

As any real hypehead knows, "Roy Ferguson" was Sir Hype's real name. Roy grew up in an average house, went to an average school, and had average friends. In many ways, Roy Ferguson was the most average Roy who'd ever Royed. That is, until he dropped out of community college to become a famous YouTuber.

Fame didn't happen immediately for Roy. At first, he tried trick-shot videos. Then, he moved on to pranks. He streamed video games, reviewed fast food, and opened baseball cards. Nothing earned more than a hundred views. Becoming famous on YouTube is hard.

But here's the thing that made Roy Ferguson different from all those other Roys: YouTube fame wasn't just a goal for him. It was his whole life. He studied video titles for an hour a day. He spent another hour every day bugging famous YouTubers to collaborate with him. When they didn't respond, he changed his email address to trick them into thinking he was important. He kept at it week after week, month after month until he finally climbed the mountain. Literally.

As fate would have it, Roy's climb to superstardom began on a literal mountain. Onacona Mountain was a hill near his house that had somehow squeaked by with the designation of "mountain" even though it was only three hundred feet high. Roy recruited his oldest buddy Ike to help him build an obstacle course up Onacona Mountain, then gathered guys from the neighborhood to race to the top. The guys ran up Slip 'N Slides, crawled through slime, and hurdled barbed wire all for a taco on top of the hill. Roy used the aforementioned email trick to convince a local taco truck to pay for the whole thing. Roy called the video, "Sir Hype's Mountain Challenge." The video earned twelve million views in its first week, and the legend of Sir Hype was born.

In the years that followed, the guys from that video became Sir Hype's best friends. They created many more challenge videos, including such masterpieces as "We Played Laser Tag in a Haunted Castle," "I Gave Away a House in a Game of Musical Chairs," and "Last One Upside Down Wins $50,000."

But Sir Hype's most popular videos were always the Mountain Challenges. Mountain Challenge Two featured trampolines up the side of a cliff. Mountain Challenge Three introduced the glitter blizzard, viper vat, and raccoon rodeo.

Mountain Challenge Four was broadcast live on ESPN and earned more viewers than the World Series and NBA Finals combined. How could Sir Hype possibly top that?

Well, Archie would find out if Mae could ever figure out how to press "record" on the camera. Sir Hype had just released a video entitled "My Next Mountain Challenge Is the Biggest Yet" twelve minutes ago, and time was ticking for Archie to upload his reaction to YouTube.

Archie aspired to one day create massive, original videos like Sir Hype, but today was not that day. Now, most of Archie's videos consisted of him filming himself watching Sir Hype's latest and greatest. Sir Hype was so popular that his fans would watch not just his videos, but also other fans watching his videos. Archie knew that if he didn't get this up soon, he'd be the last Sir Hype fan account to upload a reaction, which would be far more embarrassing than not uploading one at all. He'd be worse than those goons over at the HYPElights channel.

"You know what? Give me that." Archie snatched the camera from Mae, stacked a few books to create a homemade tripod, then pressed "record" himself. He decided to save time by skipping the usual introduction.

"What up, hypeheads?! This is Archie coming at you from Charlotte, North Carolina. The biggest video of the year just dropped. Let's get into it."

Archie clicked "play" on his mom's laptop.

"HYYYYYYYYYYPE!" Sir Hype started the video with his trademark greeting.

"HYYYYYYYYYYPE!" Archie harmonized at home.

On the video, Sir Hype spread his arms in front of his mansion's massive swimming pool. "It's the moment you've all been waiting for! Mountain Challenge Five! This one's big."

"He's going to do Everest," Archie predicted to the camera.

"Bigger than Big Time Bryce?!" Sir Hype's friend Big Time Bryce jumped into the frame. Big Time Bryce was the tallest of Sir Hype's friends at six-foot-four, making him the default enforcer of the group. Sir Hype looked Big Time Bryce up and down, smirked at the camera, then pushed Bryce into the pool.

"Hahaha!" Archie laughed a little louder than normal to play to the camera.

▶

MOUNTAIN CHALLENGE 5!!!

Sir Hype

"I've read the comments," Sir Hype continued. Fifty YouTube comments appeared on the screen. "Everest, Everest, Everest!" "We want Everest!" "Do Mount Everest, cowards!"

Archie squealed. "He's going to do it!"

"I'm going bigger than Everest," Sir Hype said. "This mountain isn't on Earth."

Archie squealed again.

"Space! It's space!" Sir Hype's buddy Yannis zoomed onto the screen. Yannis was the most divisive member of the Hype squad since he was so hyper and yappy. Sir Hype pushed Yannis into the pool too.

"Woohoo!" Archie pumped his fist for the camera. He personally had a soft spot for Yannis, but cheered to give the people what they want.

"This mountain is inside of a video game."

"HYYYYYYYYYPE!" Bryce and Yannis jumped out of the pool and joined the remaining members of the Hype Squad (three entirely interchangeable dudes named Robbie, Ronnie, and Rhodie) mobbing their leader.

While they mobbed, Archie got closer to his camera. "Guys, I'm freaking out right now. FREAKING out! I've been asking for a Sir Hype video game for years! Can you imagine how insane a Mountain Challenge video game is going to be? It's going to . . ."

"SCREEEEEECH!"

Archie stopped talking when a dragon appeared on screen. Not a guy in a dragon costume. Not a special effect. Not a robot. A real-life dragon.

Whoosh!

The dragon belched a fireball at Bryce . . .

Chomp!

. . . Swallowed Yannis whole . . .

Swoop!

. . . And flew away with the rest of the Hype Squad in its claws.

Sir Hype looked unsurprised by this development. "Oh, did I mention I'm inside the video game *right now?*" Sir Hype walked toward the camera and took it off its tripod. He then pointed it up at the sky.

The dragon was flying toward a mountain that could only exist inside of a video game. Its base formed a massive skull with a mouth that gaped open to reveal the entrance to a fiery cave. Tubes twisted around and through the mountain in what appeared to be the world's biggest waterslide. Toward the mountain's peak, gears and blades jutted from the snow at strange angles.

"Ike outdid himself with this one," Sir Hype continued. "For the first time ever, we are using Bionosoft technology to bring people inside a video game. This is the biggest Mountain Challenge yet. One hundred of my biggest fans will make it to this mountain. Only one will win the prize on top of it. Will it be you?"

The screen went black. Then, a website appeared.

MOUNTAINCHALLENGEFIVE.COM

CHAPTER TWO

HIP-E

"OK, so there's a—it's a—what do you call it when there's a ticktock, and it's ticking . . ." Archie was so overwhelmed by what he'd just seen that his brain could barely form a sentence.

"A countdown clock?" Mae offered.

"There's a countdown clock on the website!" Archie explained to the camera. "And it's at twenty-three hours and forty-six minutes, which means—which means I've got to go! Golden Arch out!"

Archie stopped the recording and turned to Mae. "I've gotta get in there."

Mae looked excited. "You can do it, Arch!"

"I've been waiting my whole life for this chance." Archie started hopping in place like a boxer preparing to step into the ring. "This is it. Whatever it takes. It's my turn now."

"Oh, actually, it's my turn." Mae hugged a tub of beads to her belly and grinned. "But after that, you'll definitely get in there!"

Archie stopped hopping. Please. Not today.

Every Tuesday afternoon, Mae would come over to help him film his Sir Hype reaction video. In return, he'd film "Arts and Crafts and Jewelry and Fun with Mae." Mae's videos were supposed to be cute little tutorials where she'd share her wealth of arts and crafts knowledge with the world. In reality, they were thirty-plus minutes of Mae stringing beads while chatting mindlessly with her big cousin. To date, Archie had filmed 247 minutes of "Arts and Crafts and Jewelry and Fun with Mae." He had yet to upload a single second to YouTube. Mae had yet to notice.

"This setup works great." Archie swiveled around the camera that was sitting on the stack of books.

"No, Arch! I need you to do it."

Archie hit record. "I'll be right back."

"Arrrrrrrch!" Mae called.

"Don't whine on camera!" Archie yelled as he ran out of his mom's office.

Archie's mind raced as he sprinted to his room. By the time that countdown clock hit zero, tens of millions of people would have viewed the video. Maybe hundreds of millions. If Archie wanted to be anywhere near the front of the line at that point, he'd need more than luck. He'd need a plan—a Roy Ferguson plan.

What would Sir Hype do?

In his room, Archie locked the door, grabbed his tablet, and pulled up his email. Archie checked this email address every day, although he'd never once received anything from it. When he started his channel, he'd bugged his mom to set up an email and website for him. He'd said that an email address would make his channel feel official. The actual purpose was a little more sneaky.

Sir Hype's email address was roy@hypestreetproductions. com. The email Archie had asked his mom to set up was roy@hipestreetproductions.com. Archie had hoped he'd get a scoop on an upcoming video from someone misspelling "hype" as "hipe" in Sir Hype's email address. That felt like something Sir Hype would have done in the early days. That plan hadn't quite worked out, but now Archie had a different use for the email.

He opened up a new message and typed "ike@ hypestreetproductions.com." Maybe if Archie could trick Ike into thinking that he was messaging Roy, he could squeeze some inside information that would help him get inside the video game first.

"Dear Ike," Archie typed before stopping. Do people start emails with "dear"? Would Sir Hype do that? He erased the greeting and started over. "Yoooooooo!" He immediately erased that too. Finally, Archie settled for the simplest message possible. "What's up with the game?"

He hit send, then started shaking. What was he thinking? Ike was a professional. He'd not only immediately see through Archie's scheme, but he'd also probably block Archie from contacting Sir Hype ever again. In one moment, Archie had ruined his relationship with his hero before it'd even begun. He'd ruined his entire future. He'd probably even ruined . . .

Ding!

One new message. Ike had already replied.

"Told you it's not a big deal. Hopping in the game right now to patch it."

Archie started shaking even more. It'd worked. It'd actually worked. He'd tricked Ike. Now what? He thought for a second, then typed "Let me see."

Send.

Archie held his breath. Every inch of his body trembled as he waited for the ding that would change his life. But instead of a ding, he got a knock.

Knock, knock, knock.

"Arch?" his mom called. "Why is Mae crying?"

"I don't know," Archie yelled back. "Ask her."

"She says you left her."

Ding!

New message from Ike. "Thought you guys were already in there? Stage site is open. Hop in." The words "Stage site" were blue. When Archie tapped the link, a new window opened.

Username: Roy

Password:

"Arch!"

"Busy, Mom! I showed her how to film herself."

"You know she doesn't care about the video," Archie's mom said. "She just wants to hang out with you."

With shaky fingers, Archie typed Sir Hype's phone password. A few years ago, the guys over at HYPElights had figured out how Sir Hype unlocks his phone by studying footage of him checking a text on camera. His password was 35006—the license plate number on his Lamborghini. Like any good hypehead, Archie had adopted the password as his own.

"ARCH!"

"Be right there, Mom."

35006

WELCOME, GAME MASTER

"Does 'right there' mean now or does it mean ten minutes?"

Archie started shaking again. "THIS IS THE MOST IMPORTANT THING THAT HAS EVER HAPPENED TO ME, MOM!" he blurted. His screen filled with all sorts of commands and graphs and gobbledygook. One large, green button at the bottom of the page caught his eye.

START GAME

Archie tapped it immediately. A large text box appeared.

OVERRIDE COUNTDOWN? THIS ACTION CANNOT BE UNDONE.

Archie tapped "YES."

REENTER PASSWORD

35006

Knock, knock, knock.

"Mom, please!"

KNOCK, KNOCK, KNOCK.

But the knocking wasn't coming from the door. It was coming from the basement.

"What's that?!" Archie's mom asked. "Mae?! Mae, are you OK?" Footsteps sprinted through the house.

The knocking got louder and louder until . . .

ZZZZzzzzzzzzwoooooo.

The power went out.

Then, the world disappeared.

CHAPTER THREE

ROBOT YANNIS

WHOOOOOSH!

Archie's whole body got sucked into something that felt like one of those cartoon tubes that twist and wind all over the place. He flipped and flopped around tight turns, long spirals, and roller-coaster hills. Finally, he *thoonked* out the other side.

Everything was black for a moment before the world slowly came into focus. Archie found himself in a house that was much different from his own. The ceiling was high. Super high. And a chandelier hung from it. Was this a foyer? Archie had never been in a house with a foyer before. Suddenly, a face appeared inches from Archie's. A face framed by pointy hair that jutted in every direction.

"YOOOOOO!"

"Yannis?" Archie croaked.

Yannis grabbed Archie's hand and yanked him off the ground. "Yo, so I'm not really Yannis. I'm like a robot. Or like artificial intelligence. Or, like, I don't know—they just put all of Yannis's words in a computer blender and then I came out. It's my job to welcome people. So . . ." Yannis looked like he lost his train of thought for a second, which didn't seem like something computers should do. Then his eyes lit up. "So, like, yoooo! You made it! How does it feel?"

Archie felt dizzy. Like he was going to throw up. He stumbled to a long glass table and squinted at Robot Yannis. Was this the video game? Or some sort of in-between place? And how long before someone found out he didn't belong? "So . . . this is it?"

"This is it!"

"I made it to the mountain challenge?"

Robot Yannis grinned. "Dope, right?"

It felt almost too good to be true. "Where's everyone else?"

"Every contestant gets their own house. This is where you'll fill out paperwork. *Thbtttt.*" Robot Yannis made a farting sound with his mouth to clarify his opinion of paperwork. "First, I need to ask if you're over eighteen."

"Oh. Uh, no, but . . ."

"Don't worry," Robot Yannis said. "We can have someone in the real world get a parent to sign off. It'll only take a few minutes. Just know that a minute of real time equals a day of video game time, so you might be here for a while. Or . . ."

Archie could see where Robot Yannis was going with this. He puffed out his chest to make himself look five years older than he was, then replied, "Yes, I am eighteen," in his deepest voice.

Robot Yannis grinned and nodded. "Dope." He gestured to the table, and piles of papers appeared. "Then you can sign these yourself."

Archie took the top paper and studied it like he imagined an adult would. The paper was a single-space jumble of "hereinafters" and "notwithstandings" that Archie couldn't possibly decipher. Robot Yannis must have noticed Archie's struggle because he took it upon himself to explain everything in the most Yannis way possible.

"Yo, don't worry, it just says, like, you might die in here, but, like, this is a video game, so obviously you won't get hurt in real life, but, like, for some reason if you did get hurt in real life, you won't sue us."

"Oh."

"Even if you die. Which—*pffff*—would never happen. But, you know, even if you did, you wouldn't sue. Or, I guess, your family wouldn't sue us. Because you'd be dead."

"Um."

"No big deal. Normal stuff."

That didn't sound like normal stuff, but Archie signed anyway. Outside of the week his class practiced signatures in third grade, he hadn't had many opportunities to sign his name, so he did his best to scribble "Archibald James Maroney" like a real professional. It looked like a kid forging his parent's signature.

Yannis slid another paper toward Archie. "This says we can record you all the time. Even when you don't want us to. Like if you're crying alone. But don't worry—you won't cry because this is going to be super fun."

"There are cameras everywhere? Like even in the bathroom?"

"DUDE! NO! You don't have to go to the bathroom in a video game."

"Really?"

"Dope, right? Also, video games don't have cameras. We can record everything from every angle at all times. Basically, you have no privacy."

Archie felt like this version of Yannis was probably not the best fit for the welcome job, but he signed anyway.

Ding!

"That sound means we're recording now." Yannis gave a cheesy grin, then pulled out more papers. "This says you can't say anything bad about Sir Hype. Ever. Because if you do, he can sue you. But don't worry—he won't because he's totally cool."

Archie quickly signed. "I would never say anything bad about Sir Hype."

Yannis slid another paper in front of Archie. "Or Hype Street Productions, LLC."

"Or Hype Street Productions, LLC," Archie confirmed as he signed.

"Or the sponsor of this video, Nabisco."

Archie signed. This was starting to feel significantly less fun than he imagined it would. "Are we done yet?"

"Yes! Wait. No." Yannis reached into his pocket and pulled out something that looked like a slap bracelet. "Wear this." He thwacked it around Archie's wrist.

"Ow!"

"You can use that to get out of the video game any time you want."

"OK."

"It's a safety thing. *Thbbbbt.*" Yannis repeated his farting sound to clarify his opinion of safety. "The government makes us do it so nobody gets trapped in a video game. Laaaaaaame."

The bracelet was completely smooth except for a clear plastic shield covering a small red button. "If I want to get home, I press this button?" Archie asked.

"Yes. It's a little bomb."

"Excuse me?"

"It blows you up into a million pieces."

"Why would I do that?!"

"To go home."

"OK, I'm not going to do that."

"Right."

Whoosh!

With that, the floor opened underneath Archie, sending him tumbling down into a dark room.

Click. Click. Click.

Lights clicked on to light up a long closet full of costumes. There were cowboy boots and astronaut helmets and baking aprons and one extra-poofy green costume that looked sort of like an avocado.

Yannis appeared in front of Archie. "Pick one that fits your personality."

Archie strolled past racks and racks of hangers. What was his personality? Certainly not an avocado. He liked Sir Hype. Maybe that was his personality? He touched a plain T-shirt with the word "HYPE" written across the chest. It disappeared off the hanger and appeared on his body.

"Dope." Yannis said. "One more step."

The ground opened again.

"WHOA!"

The bottom level of the house was a giant garage filled with every vehicle imaginable. There were Ferraris, Porsches and Lamborghinis next to buses, snowplows, and ice cream trucks. "You'll drive to the foot of the mountain where you'll meet Sir Hype," Yannis explained. "Pick your vehicle."

Archie strolled past a row of the most expensive cars in the world. He passed a taxi, tank, and limo before stopping in front of a dented 2008 Kia Rio. "This one."

The vehicle wasn't cool by any measure. It looked like it may not even turn on. But Archie recognized it as an exact replica of Sir Hype's first car. Today wasn't about looking cool or driving fast. It was about making an impression on Sir Hype.

"Ooooohkay." Yannis tossed Archie the keys.

Archie hopped in and struggled to fit the key into the ignition while desperately trying to appear like he'd driven a car before. After a *putz* and a *puff*, the engine turned over. A garage door opened in the distance.

Yannis stuck his head through Archie's window. "Oh, one more thing. Five hundred people are starting their engines right now. Only the first hundred to the mountain get to climb. Good luck!"

CHAPTER FOUR

NOT HERE TO MAKE FRIENDS

"I didn't know this was a race!" Archie screeched as he slammed the gas pedal. The car revved, but nothing happened.

"Drive, dude!" Yannis said.

Archie shifted into drive, and the Kia lurched forward. With Yannis in the rearview mirror, Archie felt free to scream as loud and squeaky as necessary.

"AHHHHHHHH!"

He weaved through the vehicles in the garage at what felt like 200 miles per hour. A quick glance at the speedometer told Archie his actual speed was only 22 mph, which had to be a mistake. He screamed through the open garage door and skidded onto an empty street. A city skyline loomed up ahead, and beyond that, the mountain. Archie gunned the engine, and the Kia responded with a whine and a gradual climb to 30 mph, then 40, then 50. Archie gripped the wheel as hard as he could. It felt like he'd just shifted into hyperdrive.

As the Kia climbed to its max speed (82 mph), Archie started loosening up. The road was wide, straight, and empty, which helped him build confidence in his driving. It also got him thinking that maybe Yannis was wrong.

Maybe there weren't 499 other racers. Maybe he'd entered the game alone after all! He leaned forward in his driver's seat and allowed himself a little smirk.

Whoosh!

Just then, a Lamborghini driven by a little girl wearing a unicorn headband passed Archie.

WHOOSH!

A tank that might belong to Batman zoomed by on the left. Then, the road merged into a superhighway, and Archie's heart sank. It felt like the entire world was headed to the mountain.

HONK-HONK, HOOOOOOONK!

Archie glanced right to see a little kid wearing one of those inflatable T. rex costumes driving a garbage truck. The kid honked again, then yanked the steering wheel to run Archie off the road. Archie tapped his brakes, causing the kid to crash through the guardrail and fly off the road.

Up ahead, the road narrowed into a tunnel. To make it into the tunnel, Archie would have to merge into one of the center lanes. He waved at the driver to his right—a girl with a flower in her hair steering a float from the Rose Parade. "Can I get in?"

The girl hunched over her steering wheel and ignored Archie.

The tunnel was approaching quickly. A semitruck bore down on Archie's bumper. Archie rolled down the window. "I NEED TO GET IN!"

The girl glanced his way, then gave her steering wheel a little wiggle, causing her float to shed rose petals all over Archie's windshield.

"SERIOUSLY?!" Archie yelled.

"Not here to make friends!" the girl replied.

Archie wanted to argue—wanted to ram her off the road—but he'd run out of time. At the last second, he swerved left and crashed down an embankment on the side of the road. He tumbled down the embankment all the way down to a service tunnel. When he finally rolled to a stop, Archie took a second to breathe. Then, he tried to flip on his headlights.

"Ba-doo-bee-doo, my baaaaabyyyy!"

Unfortunately, Archie did not turn on the headlights. Instead, he turned on the radio that happened to be playing a peppy old-time song that very much did not match his current mood.

"We cruised down the coast in my Chevrolet . . ."

Archie was running out of time, so he decided to ease onto the gas and hope for the best. He splashed through raw sewage on his way into the dark tunnel.

"... On that endless, sun-kissed hiiiiighway ..."

He used his left hand to drive and his right to search for the lights. Unfortunately, he only managed to turn the song louder.

". . . THE RADIO PLAYING OUR FAVORITE SONG ..."

It was pitch black now.

"... WITH YOU BY MY SIDE, I CAN'T GO WRONG! MY BAAAA—"

SLAM!

Archie silenced the radio by punching it. His punch also happened to turn on emergency flashing lights. Those lights illuminated the slimy tunnel walls, green trickle on the ground, and rats. Not one or two or three rats, but jillions of them, crawling all over his car. Archie tried switching on the windshield wipers, but unfortunately . . .

"MY BAAAAAAABYYYYY!"

"AHHHHHH!"

This was the moment Archie's brain decided to shut down. In a fit of madness, he decided his best course of action would be to punch the gas pedal, drive blindly, and sing along with the radio as loudly as he could.

"BA-DOO-BEE-DOO, MY BAAAAAAABYYYYY!" Archie sang while his rat-covered car sped through the video game sewer. His loud singing helped mask his nerves, but it also masked something else—the rumble of sewage behind him. Because Archie was singing about his baby, he was unprepared for the flood of yuck that was about to overtake him.

Whooooosh!

The sewer water propelled Archie through the sewers, up a ramp, and—

SPLASH!

—into the main tunnel, which also happened to be crumbling. Vehicles behind Archie swerved to avoid sewage. Vehicles in front of Archie rammed each other to avoid falling debris.

CRASH!

A chunk of rubble fell in front of Archie, blocking his path.

"This way!" a voice called over a bullhorn.

To Archie's left was a fire truck holding up a section of the tunnel. A kid in a firefighter hat waved racers through.

"Go, go, go!"

Archie sped through the gap and navigated several more pieces of debris before finally emerging from the tunnel onto a forest road. The difference between the chaos of the tunnel and the tranquility of the forest was jarring. Up here, the birds sang. The leaves were turning. Little squirrels scampered everywhere. And, at the moment, only one other vehicle was on the road.

Archie slowed as he approached a mangled parade float on the side of the road with four flat tires. The flower girl waved at him. "Help!" she yelled.

When Archie rolled down his window, the girl lit up. "Thank you!"

Archie waited until she reached for the passenger door handle before scrunching up his face. "Oh! So sorry. I'm not here to make friends." Then, he hit the gas.

Archie cackled to himself as he peeled away. That wasn't normally something he'd do, but the flower girl absolutely deserved it. He felt so great that he sang along to the song that was somehow still playing on the radio. "My baaaaaaa—YOW!"

Something pinched Archie's neck. He slapped at it and got a fistful of fur. His eyes widened.

Rat.

Somehow, one lone rat had survived the mayhem in the tunnel. That rat had clung to the car through the whole race, awaiting his invitation to enter the lavish cloth interior of the 2008 Kia Rio. That invitation came when Archie rolled open the window to taunt the flower girl.

The rat scampered across the steering wheel. Archie swatted at it.

The rat fell onto the driver's seat. Archie flailed.

The rat crawled up Archie's shirt. Archie drove straight into an oak tree.

CHAPTER FIVE

DANCE WITH DANGER

Archie stumbled out of the car. His ears rang, and his head hurt. Even though this was a video game, that crash felt very real. He tried flagging down a hot-pink Corvette. The driver—a teenage girl wearing a teddy bear costume—didn't even see him, as she was too busy fixing her makeup in the mirror. The next driver—a man wearing devil horns—went out of his way to try hitting Archie with his Nissan Altima.

Archie decided he'd have a better chance completing the race by foot. Just a few steps into his trek, he heard a familiar, squeaky voice.

"ARCH!"

No way. Archie looked back. Sure enough, there was his cousin Mae, driving a bedazzled Jeep and wearing butterfly wings. "Arch! I love this!"

Archie had two dozen questions running through his mind at that moment, but he asked the most pressing one first. "Can I have a ride?!"

"Yeah, yeah, yeah! Oh, guess what?! I made a friend! This is Naila!"

The flower girl from earlier leaned around Mae to glare at Archie from the passenger seat. Archie gulped and hopped into the backseat.

"WHEEEEEE!" Mae screamed as she took off. Mae drove exactly like every little kid drives their first Power Wheels vehicle—by jamming the pedal to the metal and twisting the steering wheel back and forth at random. Also, she wasn't quite tall enough to see over the dashboard.

Naila reached for the wheel, but Mae whacked her hand. "MY TURN!"

"We're gonna die," Naila groaned.

Archie leaned toward his cousin's ear. "How did you get here?"

"AUNT STEPH'S COMPUTER! I WAS TRYING TO DO BEADS, BUT I WAS CRYING BECAUSE YOU LEFT

ME, AND THEN AUNT STEPH'S COMPUTER MADE A FUNNY SOUND, SO I LOOKED UP, AND IT JUST WENT *THWOOOO!*" She made a vacuum sound with her mouth. "THEN I MET ROBOT YANNIS AND FOUND THIS JEEP AND . . ." Mae turned around. "YOU DID IT, ARCH! YOU REALLY DID IT!"

Archie grabbed his cousin's head and turned it back to the road.

"What did you do?" Naila asked.

"Nothing!" Archie replied. Mae turned around again to smile at him. "Watch the road!" Archie screamed.

Mae's eyes almost made it back to the road, but they stopped on Naila. "ARCH SAID HE'D DO WHATEVER IT TAKES, AND HE DID! AND I'M SO PROUD . . ."

"WATCH THE ROAD!" Both Archie and Naila shouted at the same time.

Thwoonk!

Too late. Mae ran straight into a thicket of blackberry bushes.

"Ahhhh!" Archie peeled thorns away from his face.

"Reverse!" Naila said.

"I am! It's not doing anything!" Mae replied.

Archie peeked up front. "Your foot's on the brake."

"This is how you reverse in *Mario Kart*!"

"That's it," Naila said. She ducked under a branch full of prickers and squirmed over to the driver's seat. "I've got this, thanks." Naila backed out of the bush, moved Mae to the passenger seat, squealed onto the road, then slammed the Jeep into drive.

With all Mae's fooling around, she'd lost a lot of ground in the race. Fortunately, this section of the course took place on a rough trail with gnarled roots growing across the road, which gave the Jeep a distinct advantage over all the sleek, high-performance race cars. Naila swerved around stuck vehicles and maneuvered off-road like she'd been driving this Jeep her whole life.

"Weeheehee!" Mae cheered. "You're such a good driver!" Then, she turned to Archie. "She's such a good driver!"

Archie didn't want to admit Naila was good at anything. He leaned forward and said, "Careful, you've got a seven-year-old in here."

"I'm trying to win," Naila replied. "Whatever it takes, right?" Then she laid on her horn and screamed at someone dressed in a full-body inflatable coffee mug costume. "GET OUTTA HERE, CUP!" The mug looked absolutely terrified despite the cute, little smile painted on its face.

Archie shrank back in his seat. The trees were thinning out now, revealing the mountain up ahead. Only one obstacle remained—a narrow canyon with towering walls on either side.

Naila gunned the engine and caught up to a big, long hot dog on wheels driven by a kid wearing a *Cat in the Hat* top hat. Naila sped up to pass the hot dog, but he sped up too. Naila slowed down, and he also slowed down.

"GO AHEAD!" Naila yelled.

The kid shook his head.

"WHY NOT?!"

"I DANCE WITH DANGER!"

The canyon walls were getting closer.

"WHAT DOES THAT EVEN MEAN?!"

"I DANCE WITH DANGER!" the kid repeated.

Mae leaned out the window. "I'M MAE!"

"BENNY."

"I LIKE YOUR HAT, BENNY!"

"WHAT?!"

"I LIKE YOUR . . ."

WHAM!

Naila took advantage of this small distraction to try ramming Benny. Unfortunately, his vehicle was so hefty that it held its ground while the Jeep spun out. Naila, Mae, and Archie all screamed while they entered the canyon backward. Then—

SMASH-CRASH!

Both the hot dog vehicle and the Jeep smashed into a thirty-seven-vehicle pileup. At the front of the crash, Devil Horn Guy exited his Nissan Altima and waltzed toward the finish line on foot, looking quite pleased with himself for ruining everyone else's day.

Rumble-rumble-rumble.

The earth started shaking, then ground began crumbling near the canyon's entrance. The crumbling quickly advanced toward the Jeep.

"RUN!" Archie cried.

Naila took off by herself while Archie pushed Mae out of the Jeep and on top of the hot dog. The kids joined the shrieking crowd scrambling over vehicles toward the finish line. Archie shouted coaching tips back to his cousin while he ran ahead. "Stay to the left! Now, climb up the back of the fire truck! We've got a straight shot down the fire ladder while . . . Hey, Mae? MAE?!"

"Come here, buddy boy!" Mae yelled as she dangled inside the cabin of the fire truck.

Archie pulled his cousin up. "Go!"

"He needs help!"

Archie turned to run, but Mae grabbed his sleeve. "Arch!"

Archie stuck his head inside the cab of the truck. The firefighter kid who'd helped everyone earlier was trapped underneath a toolbox. Archie grabbed his hand. "One, two, three, pull!"

The kid flopped on top of the fire truck, then leapt to the next vehicle. He turned and held out his arms to Mae. "Jump!"

By working together, Archie, Mae, and Firefighter Kid stayed one step ahead of the crumbling ground. Finally, they dove across the finish line just as the last of the canyon floor collapsed. Archie lay on the ground panting. He'd made it. He'd actually made it.

Up close, the mountain loomed so tall that it was impossible to look at it without feeling both intimidated and dizzy. From here, Archie could see that the mouth of the skull at the base of the mountain opened wide enough to swallow a skyscraper. A fiery, orange glow radiated from the skull's eyes. That was as far as Archie could see from the ground, and yet he knew from the announcement video that this was just a small fraction of the mountain.

Archie, Mae, and Firefighter Kid stood up and joined the ninety-seven other contestants who'd arrived before them marveling at the mountain. Then, a very special celebrity joined the group.

"Hyyyyyyyyyyype!" Sir Hype yelled from a nearby rock.

"Hyyyyyyyyyyype!" The crowd joined.

"Woo!" Sir Hype raised his arms above his head along with the crowd. "Now, you all have to go home."

CHAPTER SIX

WAHOO

Just like the mountain, Sir Hype looked bigger in person than he did on video. He wore a tight V-neck T-shirt that showed off the biceps he'd been working on and a beard that straddled the fine line between stylish and maybe-too-bushy. But it was the way he carried himself that made him look larger-than-life. He stood on that rock with his shoulders back and chest out just like Captain America.

The crowd stared in awe at their hero for a second before breaking out in laughter. Go home? Sir Hype had such a great sense of humor.

Sir Hype continued smiling, "I love you all. I'm so happy to see you. But there's been a mistake."

The crowd laughed louder.

Sir Hype sighed and motioned for help. People hooted and hollered when Big Time Bryce took Sir Hype's place on the rock. Then, Bryce spoke up. "Party's over!"

All hooting and all hollering ended.

Sir Hype returned to the rock. "The real challenge doesn't start until tomorrow."

"But we're here now!" a panda bear called.

"Right, because someone messed up," Sir Hype said.

"Yooooooo, who wants swag?!" Yannis chose this moment to draw attention to himself by holding up a pair of water bottles.

"SWAG!" Mae clutched Archie's arm with glee.

That was the only positive reaction to Yannis's announcement in the whole crowd. Everyone else jumped to the (very reasonable) conclusion that this must be Yannis's fault.

"What did you do?" Devil Horn Guy got in Yannis's face.

"Brought some dope swag. Here ya yo," Yannis said, substituting the word "yo" for "go" in an effort to break the tension with a cute turn of phrase.

The devil did not care for the cuteness. "Yo. Keep your bottle. And get me up that mountain."

"Yeah, fix this!" someone dressed as a soldier demanded.

People started getting in Yannis's face. The coffee mug mascot snatched the water bottle out of his hand. Then the pushing started.

Archie gulped. Of course, he knew that Yannis wasn't the problem. But he also knew that he wasn't ready for this type of attention were he to tell the truth.

Finally, someone stepped up before things could get too ugly. "I can explain what happened!"

All eyes turned back to the rock. A skinny guy was standing up there dressed in a polo shirt and indoor soccer shoes even though he looked like he'd never stepped on a soccer field in his life. He waved a tablet. "Hey, everyone,

I'm Ike. I built this mountain. I'll explain what happened, but first, I need to ask a question. Who here is from Charlotte, North Carolina?"

Archie's stomach knotted. He was from Charlotte, but he couldn't admit that now. He kept his hands glued to his side. His effort to blend in backfired when every other person in the crowd raised their hand.

"That's what I thought," Ike said. "This morning, a hacker from Charlotte breached our system."

Archie had never been called a "hacker" before. Was he going to jail?

"This hack opened a temporary portal on the main site. The five hundred people who were viewing the site nearest the hacker at the time of the breach slipped into the game. Don't worry, you're all safe. But it's time for you to go home."

"I'm not going home," Devil Horn Guy shouted.

"What's your name, sir?" Ike asked.

"Devil Doug."

"OK, Doug, here's the . . ."

"It's Devil Doug to you," Devil Doug corrected. "New Jersey Devils superfan Devil Doug. I dress up for every game. I know you've seen me on TV."

There was no way Ike had ever seen Devil Doug on TV, but he rolled with this new information to keep the conversation on track. "OK, Devil Doug. Here's the problem. Right now, this game has a memory leak. Do you know what a memory leak is?"

"Of course I know what a memory leak is!" Devil Doug scoffed with such bluster that it was clear he had no idea what a memory leak was.

"Then I'll explain for everyone else. A memory leak happens when a computer program forgets to put things back after it's done using them. It's like—do you have kids, Devil Doug?"

"I hate kids."

"OK. Well, if you had kids, you'd know that they never put their Legos back where they go. That's not a big deal if they only have a few Legos, but the more Legos they have, the bigger the problem gets. A few hundred Legos on the kitchen table make it tough to eat, a few thousand Legos on the living room floor make it hard to walk. When that number gets to a few million Legos, it's time to move to a new house."

Devil Doug crossed his arms. "I want to climb the mountain."

"Here's why that's a bad idea, Devil Doug. Your drive here used the equivalent of a few thousand Legos. That's a lot, but nothing the game can't handle. As you climb that mountain, the number of Legos you're going to use will grow exponentially. At some point, the game may no longer be able to support all those Legos. That's when the world will collapse and you will die. Do you want to die, Devil Doug?"

"I'm not going to die."

"Not right away. First, you'll notice glitches in the game. Or maybe you won't—they'll be tiny. Then, things will slow way down. It'll feel like you're walking through mud. Finally, your data will corrupt. In the real world, that last step only lasts a few seconds. In here, it'll be hours. At that point, your fate will be sealed. You will die a slow death on top of a cold mountain, praying for a hot spot to finish you off. Would you like to hear about hot spots?"

Devil Doug remained silent. He did not want to hear about hot spots. Ike's words hung in the air for a few seconds before Yannis raised his hand.

"You said you're fixing a leak?" Yannis asked.

"A memory leak, yeah."

"Like a plumber."

"Sure."

"So you're a video game plumber?"

"I guess."

"Look, everyone!" Yannis called. "It's Super Mario!"

The crowd roared with laughter, eager to move on from Ike's dire prediction. Yannis beamed. He could come up with good bits from time to time. Unfortunately, he often ran them into the ground. "Yoooooo, say 'wahoo' like Mario!"

"Not now, Yannis," Ike said.

"Wahoo! Wahoo!" Yannis chanted. Everyone else joined in.

"WAHOO! WAHOO!"

"Wahoo," Ike mumbled.

The crowd roared its approval.

"If I could have everyone's attention for one more moment!" Ike shouted.

"WAHOO! WAHOO!" the crowd chanted again.

"I'm going to need your help . . ."

"WAHOO! WAHOO!"

". . . If you could all look at your wristband . . ."

"WAHOO! WAHOO!"

". . . And lift the plastic shield . . ."

"WAHOO! WAHOO!"

Ike threw up his hands and stepped down. Sir Hype took his place on the rock. Everyone quieted immediately.

"Thank you all for your patience with this," Sir Hype said. "We'll make sure everyone gets a water bottle and six-pack of Hype Fuel when they leave. Now, who wants to demonstrate how to use their wristband?"

Nobody stepped forward.

"We'll throw in a free hoodie."

Still no one.

"Ike will say, 'wahoo.'"

Thirty hands went up.

Sir Hype brought up the little girl wearing the unicorn headband who'd been driving the Lamborghini. He gave the girl a fist bump, then Ike stepped up to the rock and did the same. "Hey!" he said. "Nervous?"

The girl gave a shy nod.

"Don't be, it's super easy. On the count of three, you're going to lift your shield, then hit your button. We'll say 'wahoo' together when you do, OK?"

The girl gave another shy nod.

"One, two, three. 'Wahoooooo!'"

The girl wahoo'ed right along and pressed her button.

"Now, wave goodbye to everyone!" Ike said. "In three seconds, you'll be safe and sound back home."

Right on cue, the girl disappeared.

"And that's all there is to it!" Ike said to the crowd. "Nothing to be afraid of. Now, let's all . . ."

"OOOoooOOOooo . . ."

The girl reappeared next to Ike all blue and wavy, kind of like a hologram. Her voice was cutting in and out. Also, she looked terrified.

"HE-CHK-EEEEE-CHK-EEEELLL-CHK-LLLLLP!" she cried.

Someone ran to help her. "No!" Ike warned. "You can't touch her!" Ike desperately typed on his tablet. "I've got it!"

CCCCRrrrrrrKKKKK-POP!

The girl disappeared again. Ike continued typing for a few more seconds, then his face turned pale. "Uh-oh."

CHAPTER SEVEN

THE ULTIMATE HOOK

"Is she OK?!" someone yelled.

Ike tapped his screen a few more times before slowly shaking his head. The crowd gasped. Someone screamed. Ike quickly tried to make things better. "I mean, she will be OK once we get out of here."

Archie felt like he was going to throw up. This was all his fault.

Mae, who had not stopped clutching Archie's arm, clutched tighter. "Arch! Are we trapped?"

"I'm gonna fix this," Archie said. "But I need you to stay right here."

Mae continued to clutch. "Where are you going?"

"I need to do this alone." Archie pried Mae off his arm and spotted Naila. He waved her over. "Can you watch her for me real quick?"

"I'm not your babysitter," Naila replied.

"NAILA!" Mae sprinted toward her new best friend, and Archie headed for the rock. He needed to come clean to Sir Hype without anyone else hearing.

To reach Sir Hype, Archie had to squeeze through a large crowd. One person he pushed past was crying. Another was hyperventilating. Devil Doug was arguing with a small child. But most people appeared to have pushed the horrific scene out of their minds and were vying for a few seconds with the legendary Sir Hype.

"Excuse me." Someone dressed like a ballerina tapped on Sir Hype's shoulder. "You were saying something about free Hype Fuel earlier, and I was wondering if I get mine."

Sir Hype smiled a very reassuring smile. "See Big Time Bryce."

"Sir Hype!" Benny yelled. "Say, 'I dance with danger!'"

"What?"

"Can you say, 'I dance with danger'? That's my catchphrase."

Sir Hype's smile wavered for just a moment before he said through clenched teeth, "I dance with danger."

"SICK!" Benny slapped Sir Hype's back.

"Get me out of here," Sir Hype mouthed to Ike.

Archie had almost reached Sir Hype, but the teenage girl dressed as a teddy bear cut in front of him. "Hiiii," she said. "My name's Kat, and I'm your biggest fan."

Sir Hype expertly switched back to smiling celebrity mode. "Hi, Kat!"

"People call me K-Bear. I want to be an influencer."

"Good for you," Sir Hype said. "It's the best job in the world."

"I was just thinking that since we're both here, we might be able to collab on . . ."

"Oh, K-Bear. I don't do collabs."

"Totally," K-Bear said. "Literally, that's fine, I just . . ." Her eyes started watering. "I want this so bad. So, so bad. I do all the trends, and . . ."

"K-Bear." Sir Hype locked eyes with the aspiring influencer. He spoke the next words as if they were the most important he'd ever utter. "Don't worry about the trends. Your videos need a great hook, great storytelling, and a great payoff. Show me someone who gets those three things—really *gets* them—and I'll show you the next famous influencer."

K-Bear put her hand over her mouth. "That's, like, so inspiring."

"You can do it K-Bear."

K-Bear gave Sir Hype a big, fuzzy hug. "Can I get a picture?"

"You don't have your phone."

K-Bear's face dropped. "No phone?"

"Not until you leave."

K-Bear's eyes darted back and forth. She looked like she wanted to scream. "Get us out of here."

"I'm working on it."

A greasy guy dressed as a wizard tried slipping in next, but Archie pushed past him. "Hey," Archie said. "I—uh . . ."

"A month," Ike interrupted.

Sir Hype swiveled his head. "What?"

"A month until someone notices us. Maybe two."

"What does that mean?"

"You know how a day in a video game is just one minute in the real world? The rest of the development team is grabbing dinner right now. That's at least a half hour."

"But you're getting me out of here now." Sir Hype interrupted.

"I can't."

"You will."

"The wristbands aren't working," Ike calmly explained. "The only person authorized to leave is the Game Master."

"But I'm the Game Master," Sir Hype said.

"Not today. The person who started the game is the Game Master."

"Didn't you start the game?"

"Excuse me." Firefighter Kid tapped Sir Hype on the shoulder.

Sir Hype grimaced for just a microsecond before forcing a giant smile and turning to greet one of his fans. "Hey, buddy! I just need a minute, OK?"

"That's fine," the kid said. "Just wanted to say thanks for letting me come here today."

"My pleasure!" Sir Hype responded.

"I was in a car accident a couple years ago, and I haven't been able to walk since. It's, um, really cool to walk again. So thanks."

"Wait, you weren't able to walk, but now you can?"

"Inside the video game, yeah."

"What's your name?"

"Jin-Soo."

"Jin-Soo, would you like me to autograph your fire helmet?"

"Um, OK?" Jin-Soo said.

Sir Hype held out his hand, which was Ike's cue to roll his eyes and hand over a pen. Sir Hype signed the helmet and patted Jin-Soo on the head to send him on his way.

"Great story," Sir Hype said as he handed Ike his pen back. "It's a tragedy we won't get to use it."

"A true tragedy," Ike mumbled.

Archie waved his hand to get Sir Hype's attention. "Hi," he said.

"Wait a second." Sir Hype's eyes lit up. "What if we *can* use it?"

"So I think I know why everyone's in here," Archie continued in hopes that maybe he could get Sir Hype's attention if he just kept talking.

"The winner's portal on top of the mountain," Sir Hype said. "That's still open, right?"

"Probably," Ike replied.

Archie raised his voice. "Um, Ike got an email earlier from someone . . ."

Sir Hype continued ignoring Archie. "So if someone reaches that portal—that's it, right? Everyone gets sucked out of the game? Even the people who've already died?"

"Or the game breaks," Ike said.

"The ultimate hook." Sir Hype smiled his most genuine smile yet.

Archie couldn't let this go any longer. He finally got between Sir Hype and Ike and yelled, "I'M THE HACKER!"

CHAPTER EIGHT

MISTAKES AND STORIES

Sir Hype's eyes widened.

"I'm really sorry," Archie said. "This is all my fault. If I would have known . . ."

"Have you told anyone else?" Sir Hype asked.

Archie shook his head.

Sir Hype grabbed Archie's arm. "We need to talk." He led Archie toward an ice cream truck.

Ike tagged along too. "Don't worry, you're not in trouble," Ike said. "You can actually help everyone escape."

Sir Hype hopped into the ice cream truck with Archie, then stopped Ike before he could come in too. "Keep the crowd away for a few minutes." Inside the ice cream truck, Sir Hype grabbed himself a red, white, and blue Bomb Pop and handed Archie an ice cream sandwich. "So," he said, taking a big lick. "You're the hacker."

"I-I-I didn't think it was hacking!" Archie's whole body shook. This was not the way he'd imagined meeting his hero. "I'm sorry—I just sent an email!"

"Wait," Sir Hype said. "You used my email trick on Ike?"

"I spelled 'hype' with an 'i.'"

Sir Hype laughed and laughed.

"I promise I didn't know this would happen. I just wanted to meet you."

"Well, now you've met me. I'm Roy. What's your name?"

"Archie."

"What did you want to tell me, Archie?"

"I'm sorry."

Sir Hype suddenly got serious. "Stop using that word."

"OK, sorry."

"Let me ask you something. Have you ever heard me apologize?"

Archie shrugged.

"I thought you were a superfan. Have you ever heard me apologize?"

Archie shook his head.

"I've had time to reflect on my actions, and I am deeply sorry for the harm I have caused . . ." Sir Hype briefly switched to a mocking tone while reciting a typical YouTube apology. "Archie, you will never hear me apologize—not because I never make a mistake, but because I am a storyteller. Storytellers take mistakes and turn them into better stories. Do you want to make mistakes or make stories?"

"Stories," Archie quickly replied.

"In just a moment, Ike will ask you to leave the game. He'll hand you the phone number of someone who'll get the rest of us out. Archie, you have a choice. You can take that number and be a hero to everyone in here. Or, you can tear up that number and be a hero to the entire world."

"But I thought . . . Don't you want to get out?"

"We all get out—me, you, the unicorn girl, everyone who's already died—if one person reaches the top of the mountain." Sir Hype held up one finger to make his point, then pointed that finger at Archie. "You can help create the greatest YouTube video of all time. Think about it. It's the ultimate mountain challenge. This time, it's not about money. It's about survival. This time, there are real stakes."

Archie nodded.

"We've got the best hook. The best story. And then, there's the payoff. Archie, can you imagine the moment you reach the mountain peak and rescue everyone? Your life will never be the same."

Archie started to nod, then remembered his cousin. "But the memory leak . . ."

". . . Is something we'll use to make the story feel more exciting," Sir Hype interrupted. "But between you and me, it's not real. Do you know how often Ike comes to me with this stuff? If I stopped filming every time Ike got scared, I wouldn't have a single video. I built this mountain. I know it better than anyone else. Stick with me, and I'll keep you safe."

Archie nodded.

Sir Hype smiled. "Hyyyyyyyy . . ."

". . . YYYYYYPE!" Archie joined in.

"This is gonna be sick!" Sir Hype attempted a cool-guy handshake that Archie absolutely botched. Then, he threw away the rest of his Bomb Pop and bounded out the door. Archie followed his lead.

Ike caught Archie outside the ice cream truck. "You did the right thing by coming forward." He pressed a piece of paper into Archie's hand. "This is Victor Esmail's phone number. In just a minute, you're going to press the button on your wristband. Don't worry—your button works. It's the only one that does. As soon as you get out, call Victor and tell him I said to start the emergency extraction. Victor's going to . . ."

"Attention, please!" Sir Hype yelled. He'd climbed on top of the ice cream truck so everyone could get a better view. "I have a question for everyone. Who wants to make the greatest video of all time?!"

Every hand in the crowd went up.

"Hold on, what's he doing?" Ike asked Archie. Archie responded with a grin.

"No one on earth has spent more time studying YouTube than I have," Sir Hype continued. "And if I know anything, it's this: we are about to create the most viewed video in human history."

"Sorry, I've got to step in here real quick." Ike ran for the ice cream truck.

"We are going to climb that mountain," Sir Hype said. "And at the top, we will escape. Will there be danger?" He pointed to Ike, who'd just flopped onto the truck's hood.

"Yes!" Ike wheezed. "Real danger! The memory leak . . ."

"Real danger," Sir Hype repeated. "This mountain challenge is the toughest yet. Some might not make it to the top. But that's OK, because we just need one person to reach the peak."

"We actually don't," Ike said. "We just need to wait here."

"And how long did you tell me we'd need to wait?"

"Earlier, I said a month or two, but now that . . ."

"BOOOOOO!" The crowd drowned out the rest of his sentence.

"Where's Jin-Soo?" Sir Hype asked.

Jin-Soo raised his hand from the middle of the crowd.

"Come on up here." While Jin-Soo approached the ice cream truck, Sir Hype shared his story with the group. "My new friend Jin-Soo was in a wheelchair yesterday. But today—right here in this video game—he can walk. Isn't that incredible?"

The crowd cheered while Sir Hype helped Jin-Soo on top of the ice cream truck. "Jin-Soo, you're an inspiration to all of us. Let me ask you something—do you want to climb?"

Jin-Soo blushed and nodded.

Sir Hype turned back to the crowd. "You can stay back here with Ike if you want, but I'm looking for some legends. I'm looking for another Jin-Soo. Who here wants to make history?"

"HYYYYYYYPE!" The crowd roared so loud that the ground shook.

Sir Hype smiled a deeply contented smile while he surveyed the crowd. His eyes ended up on Archie. He winked. Archie winked back. Then, Archie tore up the phone number.

CHAPTER NINE

ONE-TWO—OOF

Sir Hype climbed off the ice cream truck and led the group toward the skull at the base of the mountain. Archie tried squeezing toward the front of the line, but got pushed backward. A hand grabbed his arm.

"Arch!" Mae said. She now wore Naila's flower in her hair. "I don't want to go in the scary face!"

"It's OK." Archie gave his cousin a little hug. "I'll keep you safe."

Naila caught up with Archie. "Didn't know you were besties with Sir Hype."

Archie shrugged. "That's what happens when you're here to make friends."

Naila rolled her eyes. "What did he say?"

"He said to throw you off the mountain."

Mae gasped. "Reeeeally?!"

"Uh, no," Archie replied.

"Then what did he say?" Mae pestered.

Archie got down on one knee so his head was right next to Mae's. "He said that we could trust him. He said that we'll have fun. And as long as we stick close to him, he won't let anything happen to us."

Mae nodded, then looked up at the approaching skull and shrunk back a little.

"Just hold my hand," Archie said. Mae was already holding Archie's hand, so she squeezed tighter as they stepped through the skull's open mouth.

Inside the skull was a massive hexagon-shaped cavern. Spotlights that hung from the cavern's domed ceiling lit up the thousands of hexagon stone tiles that made up its floor. As soon as the last person stepped into the cavern, a stone gate sealed off the entrance. Mae squeezed Archie's hand so tight that he could feel his bones squishing together.

"Listen up, everyone," Sir Hype said. "There's only one way to get out of here now." He pointed to the ceiling. Archie squinted until he spotted the opening of a massive tube situated among all the spotlights. "One minute after the challenge begins, that will turn on and suck us all up into the mountain. So we all just need to survive for one minute. Everyone with me?"

Lots of head nodding.

Sir Hype pointed at the ground. "There's lava down there. Lots of lava. Once the challenge starts, you can stand on a tile for three seconds before you fall into lava."

People shifted nervously.

"This isn't a contest anymore," Sir Hype said. "We're all in this together. If we work as a team to eliminate as few tiles as possible, we can all survive the full minute. Any questions?"

K-Bear raised her hand. "Yeah, what if we, like, die?"

"Normally, you'd go back home," Sir Hype responded. "Today—well—you saw that unicorn girl, right?"

K-Bear's eyes widened.

"She's not dead," Sir Hype quickly pointed out. "You won't be dead either. You'll just be trapped in the code, waiting for someone to reach the top of the mountain."

"But will it hurt?"

"Did it look like it hurt?"

K-Bear nodded.

"Then I guess you shouldn't fall in the lava. Now, everyone get to the wall."

The contestants all lined up against the wall, pushing and shoving to stand closest to Sir Hype. "Very good," Sir Hype said once everyone had lined up. "We're going to step forward every time I say 'step.' Do not move until I give the word."

"Yo, let's goooooo!" Yannis zoomed across a bunch of tiles with his arms outstretched.

Sir Hype briefly looked like he was reconsidering the wisdom of this decision, but forged ahead anyway. "Are we recording, Ike?"

"Have been this whole time," Ike replied with a sigh.

"Then the challenge starts on my word. Three! Two! One! Go!"

Nothing happened.

"Go!" Sir Hype yelled again.

"Only the Game Master can begin challenges," Ike explained. Then, he looked directly at Archie.

Sir Hype jumped in to protect Archie's secret. "No problem," he said. "We're all going to start it together, then. Ready?"

The crowd responded by yelling, "Three, two, one, GO!" in unison.

As soon as Archie said, "go," a horn sounded and a holographic countdown clock appeared overhead. One minute remaining.

"One-two-step!" Sir Hype called.

Everyone stepped forward and a whole row of tiles fell into boiling lava. Fifty-seven seconds remaining.

"One-two-step!"

Another step. So far, so good. Fifty-four seconds remaining.

"One-two-step!"

The whole crowd started calling out the time together. Fifty-one seconds remaining.

"ONE-TWO-STEP!"

The crowd chanted louder. People held hands. Forty-eight seconds remaining.

"ONE-TWO-STEP!"

For the first time since she'd stepped into the cavern, Mae started smiling. Archie relaxed too. He gave Mae's hand a little squeeze. Sir Hype was right, this was fun. Forty-five seconds remaining.

"ONE-TWO—OOF!"

The fun ended at exactly forty-two seconds. That is when the cup fell.

The coffee mug mascot, who'd wedged itself in the middle of the line between Sir Hype and Big Time Bryce, tripped over its ridiculous, inflatable legs. It would have been a shame to lose the mug—its innocent smile had brought joy to so many. Unfortunately, an even bigger shame occurred when the mug chose to save itself. Instead of falling down into the lava, it rolled ahead onto the next line of tiles.

"Wait!" Sir Hype called.

But the cup was not done. Oh no, it kept rolling forward, triggering a long line of tiles to crash into the lava.

Contestants that were counting on those tiles had only two seconds to choose a new direction. They did not handle that choice with grace.

"AHHHHHH!"

They sprinted in every direction. As those people stepped in front of other contestants, the panic spread until everyone was running wild.

Splash!

A mermaid was the first to fall into the lava.

Splash!

A vampire went next.

Splash, splash, splash!

Contestants started dropping left and right.

"Hold my hand!" Archie yelled to Mae as he tried to chart a clear course.

"EEEEEE!" Mae squealed. She clutched Archie's arm with both hands, which meant he was now trying to survive with a sixty-pound anchor tied to his arm.

Already, people had turned the middle of the cavern into swiss cheese. Archie spotted an untouched corner near the far wall. If he could just get over there, they could survive . . .

"Ahahaha!"

Archie heard Devil Doug before he saw him. By the time he located Devil Doug, it was too late—Devil Doug had already stepped on his next tile. Archie pulled Mae close to his body and dove right.

The pair crashed safely onto a neighboring tile, but now found themselves lying on the ground with only two seconds to reach the next tile. Still holding on to Mae, Archie rolled over to get a fresh three seconds. Maybe Archie could just roll out the clock.

"Ahahaha!"

Just as Archie had that thought, Devil Doug took out the next row of tiles. Only one option left—Archie threw Mae across the gap.

"Run!" he yelled.

"Arch!"

"RUUUUN!"

Just before Mae's tile fell into the lava, Naila pulled her to safety.

"Take care of her!" Archie yelled as he hopped across a checkerboard pattern of tiles. He glanced up at the clock. Twenty-three seconds remained. It seemed impossible that such little time had passed. Archie finally found a clear block of tiles where he could slow down and take in the scene.

Sir Hype had employed Big Time Bryce as his bodyguard to keep people away from his tiles. K-Bear had chosen the strategy of jumping onto people's backs and screaming. Somehow, the coffee mug was still rolling. Naila had brought Mae over to a small island of kids she'd organized with Jin-Soo. They were surviving with the one-two-step strategy.

Things started feeling more organized because most of the people who'd been running in blind panic had already fallen into lava. Really, there was only one such person left.

"Yoooooooo . . ." Yannis screamed his head off as he sprinted past Archie.

". . . ooooooooo . . ." He crashed into a flight attendant, knocking her into the lava.

". . . ooooooooo . . ." And he headed straight toward the island of kids. Archie looked at the clock. Ten seconds left. That was plenty of time for Yannis to gobble up all the kids' blocks.

". . . oooOOOOO . . ." Yannis screamed louder to give himself extra strength as he jumped over a pit of lava toward the island of kids.

". . . OOOOO—OOF!"

Naila turned Yannis's "yo" into an "oof" by throwing a shoulder into him just as he reached the island. Yannis tumbled backward into the lava.

Three.

Two.

One.

WHOOSH!

All remaining contestants got sucked up the tube.

CHAPTER TEN

LET'S A-GO!

Archie got sucked into the tube along with everyone else. He twisted and turned inside the lava shaft as it snaked around inside the mountain. Finally—

Thoonk!

The tube spit him out with such force that he flew ten feet into the air. Archie curled into a ball to protect himself for the landing, but there was no need—he *poomf*ed into a fluffy snow bank. Archie stood slowly and brushed himself off. The group had moved much higher up the mountain to a snow-filled plateau filled with hills, bunkers, and igloos. It looked like some sort of arena.

"WeeeeeEEEEE!"

A screaming missile flew through the air before plopping next to Archie. It was Mae. "ARCH! WE MADE IT!" She gave him a cold, wet hug. Then, Mae gasped. "Snow?" She whipped her head back and forth before looking up. "SNOW! IT'S SNOWING!"

Mae gathered a bunch of snow into a clump and offered it to Archie. "Snow cone?" Archie shook his head, so Mae shoved the snow into her mouth. "THIS IS THE BEST DAY

EVER!" Mae leaped to her feet and ran through the arena. "HEY, EVERYBODY! IT'S SNOWING!" She tripped over the coffee mug, who was lying on the ground making snow angels, then continued sprinting. "WHO WANTS A SNOW CONE?!"

Naila, who was walking from the other direction, stopped and bent over the mug. "Proud of yourself, cup?" she asked sarcastically. The mug paused its snow angel until Naila turned her anger elsewhere. "Hey!" she yelled when she spotted Archie. "I told you that I'm not a babysitter."

Archie stood up and brushed himself off. "Thanks for taking care of Mae back there."

"I mean it," Naila said. "She's your problem."

"I know."

Naila stepped closer. She could get pretty intimidating when she wanted to. "Because next time . . ."

"Well, look who it is!" Sir Hype interrupted.

Archie smiled because he was going to get a chance to show off his new best-friend status with Sir Hype. Unfortunately, Sir Hype wasn't coming for Archie. He gave a fist bump to Naila instead. "I saw what you did back there."

Naila, who'd been acting real tough just a moment ago, shrunk. "I'm really sorry about Yannis—I didn't mean to . . ."

"Don't apologize," Sir Hype said. "You understand story."

"I—um—what?"

"A random mermaid goes down? Who cares. We never met her. That cup over there—" Sir Hype pointed to the mug, who was still trying to perfect its snow angel form. "No one cares about that cup. But people know Yannis. People root for Yannis. Eliminating Yannis shows people this is for real. Nice job." Sir Hype gave Naila another fist bump.

Before a blushing Naila could respond, Ike pulled Sir Hype away. "You've gotta call this off."

Sir Hype looked at the sky, then stuck out his tongue. When a snowflake fell on it, he smacked his lips, then turned to Ike. "It's snowing. Is it supposed to be snowing?"

"Yes."

Sir Hype hopped in place. "Ground is solid." He poked Ike. "You're solid. Seems like everything's working fine."

"We just lost twenty-four people!"

"And how many were we supposed to lose?"

"Zero! You just told everyone zero!"

"In the original design for the game. How many were we supposed to lose during the first challenge?"

Ike refused to answer.

Sir Hype poked Ike again. "How could you forget so soon?"

Ike crossed his arms in front of his chest.

"Twenty-four," Sir Hype whispered. "Say it with me. Twenty-four. Twenty-four. Twenty-four. It's perfect, Ike. Everything's perfect." Sir Hype winked at Ike, then stood on top of an igloo and addressed the crowd. "HYYYYYYYYYYYPE!"

Everyone responded with a "hype" of their own.

"I'm standing among legends," Sir Hype said. "Absolute legends. It got gnarly back there, but you all kept your heads, and now look at you. Give yourselves a round of applause."

The crowd went wild. While everyone was busy congratulating themselves, Ike took Archie aside. "You've gotta go back."

Archie tried pulling away. "I want to hear what happens next."

"Nothing! Nothing's going to happen next if you let this continue."

"Everything's working fine," Archie said.

"Yes. Until it's not."

"That's when I'll go back."

"Why?" Ike asked. "Why would you do this?" He glanced at Sir Hype who was still hyping up the crowd.

"I know why he's doing it, but why would you risk your life for this? And that girl—is she your sister? Why would you risk her life for this?"

"She's not my . . ."

"Is this guy bothering you?" Sir Hype hopped down from his igloo to step between Archie and Ike. He poked Ike's belly playfully.

"Nawww," Archie said, despite never having used the word "naw" in his life. "It's just Ike being Ike."

"Hey, I didn't see much of you during that last challenge," Sir Hype said to Archie. "I want you to be a star out there. If people don't see you, they forget about you."

Archie nodded.

"I feel like I'm going crazy," Ike said. "This memory leak is a problem. A BIG problem."

"And whose problem is it?" Sir Hype asked.

"It's all of our problem!"

Sir Hype shook his head. "You're the one who got tricked by a ten-year-old's email."

Archie was thirteen years old, actually, but he wasn't about to correct Sir Hype.

"You're the plumber," Sir Hype said. "So do what plumbers do. Find the leak. Fix the leak."

Ike bit his lip. He looked furious.

"Time's wasting." Sir Hype smiled and switched to his Super Mario voice. "Let's-a-go!"

Ike clenched his jaw.

Sir Hype elbowed Archie and did the voice again. "Let's-a-go!"

Archie felt bad about taunting Ike, but he did have a great Mario impression that he'd love to show Sir Hype. "Let's-a-go!" Archie repeated.

HOOOOOOONK!

An airhorn sounded, causing Archie to jump a foot into the air.

Ike turned to Archie. "Well done," he said sarcastically.

"Me?! What did I do?"

"You started the next challenge."

"No, I didn't!"

"You said, 'go.'"

CHAPTER ELEVEN

CHESTNUT

A red jersey magically appeared on Archie. Sir Hype and Ike got red jerseys too.

"What is this?!" Archie asked.

Ike rolled his eyes and looked at Sir Hype. "Want to explain to the group before someone gets hurt?"

Sir Hype jumped back onto the igloo. When the crowd saw him up there, they started the usual greeting of "Hyyyyyyy . . ."

Sir Hype cut them off mid-hype. "The next challenge started a little early," he said pointing to the sky.

The holographic countdown clock was back. This time, it was joined by two other words: "RED" and "GREEN." Those colors matched the team jerseys. Everyone on Archie's side of the arena wore red, and all contestants on the other side wore green.

"This is a five-minute snowball fight," Sir Hype explained. "Three hits and you're out. Whichever team has the most points at the end gets to move on. Now, everyone can survive if we . . ."

Piff!

All eyes turned to Devil Doug, who'd just chucked a snowball at a small boy wearing a green jersey and a too-big construction helmet.

RED 1, GREEN 0

The countdown clock began: five minutes remaining.

Sir Hype tried again. "We all get to survive if . . ."

Piff!

Devil Doug cackled as he pelted another little kid on the green team.

RED: 2, GREEN: 0

"Real quick," Sir Hype tried one more time. "If we all work together, we can . . ."

"AHHHHHHH!" A leprechaun charged at Devil Doug. Halfway through his charge, he stepped on a hidden land mine.

KABOOM!

The explosion covered him in snow, instantly handing him three strikes. The leprechaun transformed into a cute, cartoony ghost and floated up to a set of bleachers carved into the mountain.

RED: 5, GREEN: 0

Whatever hope Sir Hype had of finishing his sentence exploded with that mine. The arena instantly devolved into one of those old battles where soldiers from both sides charge at each other with no plan beyond screaming their brains out. Ike turned to Archie. "Under no circumstances should you . . ."

Ike got blasted with three snowballs before he could finish his sentence. Archie ran away to avoid the same fate.

THUNK! THUNK! THUNK!

Grapefruit-sized snowballs flew over Archie's head and exploded when they hit the ground. He turned around to see Hype Squad member Ronnie following him with a snow grenade launcher. Archie dove behind an ice wall and tried to make peace.

"Ronnie! What do you think about calling a truce?"

"I'M NOT RONNIE! I'M ROBBIE!"

KABOOM!

The ice wall exploded, and Archie sprinted wildly. In the middle of his panic, something caught his eye. He wasn't quite sure what it was, but it glowed like a video game prize, so he dove on it. Suddenly, a cannister with a long nozzle appeared on his back.

Pewpewpew! Pewpewpew!

It started spitting out snowballs at an incredible rate. Archie turned the nozzle toward Robbie.

Pewpewpew!

One-two-three strikes, you're out. Archie smiled. Time to be a star.

Pewpewpew!

He quickly took out a punk rocker.

Pewpewpew!

Then, a shark. (Or at least a dude wearing a shark head.)

Pewpewpew! Pewpewpew! Pewpewpew!

Archie was unstoppable! He might single-handedly win the whole thing for the red team. Where was Sir Hype? He'd be so proud.

Pewpew—brooooooooooop.

Archie's power-up disappeared in the middle of battle. He stood there unarmed and exposed, and the green team took advantage.

Poof.

One hit.

Poof.

Two hits.

Archie dove to the ground and struggled to form a snowball while he waited for his third hit. Instead, he got saved by an unlikely ally.

"GET 'EM OFF, GET 'EM OFF, GET 'EM OFF!"

K-Bear, a member of the green team, ran through the battlefield with ice swords stuck to both arms. She appeared to very much not want ice swords stuck to both arms. She spun and flailed and wreaked absolute havoc. Everything she touched—including her own teammates—froze in place.

Archie waited until the whirling ice tornado passed, then crawled into an igloo so tiny only a kid could fit inside. Unfortunately, a kid was already inside—Naila, who was on the red team.

"Have you seen Mae?" Archie asked.

"Not your babysitter."

"Whatever. Let's go, we need your help."

Naila shook her head. "Check out the score."

Archie stuck his head out of the igloo.

RED: 104, GREEN: 56

"OK, great. We're winning. But it's a snowball fight. So we need to fight."

"No, we need to survive," Naila replied.

Archie tried inspiring with his best Sir Hype impression. "Do you want to be a star, or do you want to be forgotten?"

"I just wanna get outta here, thanks," Naila said with a sarcastic smile.

Archie rolled his eyes and crawled back out of the igloo. He glanced back up at the scoreboard.

RED: 149, GREEN: 58

Then, he spotted the reason for the lopsided score. Sir Hype had found the best spot in the arena—a fortress built on top of a hill. Rhodie and (apparently) Ronnie were delivering him weapons, which he used to rain terror on every member of the green team.

"Hey!" Archie waved to get Sir Hype's attention. "How can I help?"

"Take the cannon!" Sir Hype yelled back.

Archie scanned the battlefield. The snowstorm had picked up, which was making it harder to see.

"What cannon?"

"That one! Right . . ."

KAPOW!

The cannon fired. Sir Hype's eyes widened. "Chestnut!" he screamed. Sir Hype often made up phrases he could use instead of curse words to keep his channel family friendly. This appeared to be one of those times. "CHESTNUT, CHESTNUT, CHEST . . ."

SMASH!

The hill was gone. The fortress was gone. Ronnie and Rhodie were gone. Sir Hype was gone too. Who could have caused such destruction? The smoke cleared a few seconds later, revealing the cannon's operator. It was little Mae, wearing a green jersey.

"I DIDN'T MEAN IT!" Mae yelled. "CAN YOU PLEASE COME BACK, MR. HYPE?!"

As soon as Sir Hype reached the bleachers, he marched over to Ike and started yelling. Ike shook his head and pointed at Archie.

"It wasn't me!" Archie squawked.

Sir Hype took a seat and pouted with his head in his hands. He'd soon be joined by many of his red teammates. After Mae's blast, the green team earned a string of superpowered weapons. First, there was the blizzard bazooka, then the tectonic tank, and finally . . . was that Big Time Bryce in a yeti mech suit?

Hissssss.

Big Time Bryce froze a pair of gym bros wearing too-tight tank tops with frost breath.

RED: 173, GREEN: 119

Kapoomf! Kapoomf!

Big Time Bryce squashed Jin-Soo and his battalion of little kids with snow boulders.

RED: 173, GREEN: 167

Devil Doug had seen enough. He grabbed the coffee mug mascot and used it as a big, inflatable shield as he charged Big Time Bryce.

Swoooosh!

One icicle missile was enough to take both of them out.

RED: 173, GREEN: 173

"STOP!" Sir Hype yelled from the bleachers.

"I'll never stop!" Benny yelled back from the arena. "I DANCE WITH DANGER!"

Big Time Bryce clenched his yeti fist. He was happy to dance.

"NO!" Sir Hype commanded. "We have a tied score! This is how everyone wins."

Every contestant remaining in the arena looked at each other. There weren't many of them. The red team had Archie, Naila, and Benny. The green team was composed of Big Time Bryce, K-Bear, and Mae.

"Let the clock run out, and we all get to move on," Sir Hype explained.

Everyone breathed a sigh of relief. K-Bear collapsed in the snow. Mae ran to hug her cousin. Archie kept one wary eye on Big Time Bryce and one on the countdown clock.

Three. Two. One. Zero.

A cheer erupted from the bleachers. That cheer was quickly silenced when the numbers were replaced by two words:

SUDDEN DEATH

CHAPTER TWELVE

SUDDEN DEATH

Sir Hype's eyes widened. "Ike! You said we got rid of sudden death!"

Ike clenched his jaw and pecked at his tablet.

The arena started trembling. "What do we do?" Naila shouted at the bleachers.

The arena started shaking so badly that it knocked all six contestants to the ground. Then, it broke free from the mountain and started floating in the air. "WHAT DO WE DO?!" Naila repeated.

"Get to the middle of the arena!" Sir Hype shouted.

Everyone scrunched in the middle of the arena while its edges crumbled away. Rocks tumbled hundreds of feet before smashing to the ground. The crumbling steadily closed in on the contestants.

"Ike!" Archie yelled. "Shut this off! Please!"

Ike looked up from his tablet just long enough to glare at Archie, then went back to pecking.

KkkkkrrrrrrRRRRRK!

Just then, a pair of ice swords grew from everyone's arms.

"NoooooOOOOOO!" K-Bear started her flailing and running routine again. Naila was having none of it. Before K-Bear could take out the entire red team, Naila slid under her blade, spun around, and sliced her ankle.

SHING!

K-Bear turned into a block of ice and slid across the snow to the edge of the arena. Everyone gasped. Then, the ground crumbled underneath her. The aspiring influencer tumbled into the bottomless pit before transforming into a ghost and moving to the bleachers. Now, it was three-on-two.

"I DANCE WITH DANGER!"

Benny charged at Big Time Bryce, who made quick work of him. Two-on-two.

"I don't like this, Arch," Mae said. She tried to hug her cousin, but Archie spun away just in time.

"You've gotta stay away, Mae!"

Naila pointed at Big Time Bryce with her sword. He clapped his two ice swords together. Bring it on. She charged at him, then tried the same slide attack she'd used on K-Bear. Big Time Bryce blocked it by planting one of his swords in the ground.

Mae started whimpering.

"Stay behind me," Archie said. "I'll keep you safe."

As Naila slid, she jammed her own sword into the ground, then pole-vaulted up into the air. Big Time Bryce swung at her while she flew over his head, but she dodged with a midair twist. Finally—

SHING!

Naila froze Big Time Bryce with a backstab. The arena's edge crumbled away, taking the frozen Brycicle down with it. Two-on-one. Naila turned toward the last remaining member of the green team.

Archie spread his arms to protect his cousin. "We're not doing this."

"Outta my way," Naila said as she marched closer to Mae. The edge of the arena crumbled behind her.

Archie shook his head. "You know you can't do this."

"I know I'll do whatever it takes to move on," Naila said.

"We can all move on," Archie replied. Mae squealed behind him as the crumbling arena almost took her down.

"One more chance," Naila said. "Outta my—"

SHING!

Archie struck first. He lunged at his own teammate, turning her into a block of ice before she could reach Mae. Naila's face froze with her mouth and eyes open wide in surprise. Then, the ground crumbled beneath her feet. It was down to just Archie and Mae.

Archie looked up at the bleachers. "Ike! You've gotta stop this!"

"You're the only one who can stop this!" Ike replied.

Mae bawled. The arena was so small now that she had to stand back-to-back with Archie.

"I'm not doing it," Archie said.

"Then you both die," Sir Hype shouted.

Archie squeezed his eyes closed to think.

"If you both die, then we all die!" Sir Hype yelled.

The remaining chunk of the arena began rumbling. "Please," Archie begged his cousin. "Freeze me."

Mae shook her head over and over. "Nononono."

The ground rumbled harder.

"MAE!"

"NONONONO!"

"Do the right thing!" Sir Hype yelled.

"Is she gonna be OK?" Archie yelled back.

"Do it!"

"IS SHE GONNA BE OK?!"

"Yes! Do it!"

"I'm sorry!" Archie shouted. Then, he spun around and froze Mae.

CHAPTER THIRTEEN

GORDO THE GORILLA

The arena stopped rumbling immediately after Mae tumbled into the pit. Then, the green team's bleachers crumbled.

"AHHHHHhhhhhh!" The entire team tumbled into the abyss.

After that, the single remaining rock of the arena floated over to the red bleachers, rejoining Archie with his team. A path appeared from the bleachers to the mountain trail, and everyone slowly shuffled past Archie as he hung his head and shivered. The last two people past Archie were Sir Hype and Ike. Sir Hype was trying to peek over Ike's shoulder at the tablet.

"How many left?" Sir Hype asked.

"Thirty two," Ike whispered.

Sir Hype nodded. "Right on track." Then he put his arm around Archie. "Hey, buddy. That was tough, huh?"

A tear slid down Archie's cheek.

"How do you feel?" Sir Hype asked gently.

"I just—I just wish I'd never . . ."

"Actually, would you mind lifting your head while you talk?" Sir Hype asked. "So we can see your eyes."

"Who's 'we'?"

"The audience. This is going to be a powerful moment, so I want to make sure we get a good, clean shot of it."

Archie didn't feel like repeating himself, so he hung his head again.

"Cheer up," Sir Hype said. "We'd all be dead if it weren't for you. By doing what you did, you actually saved her. Look at me."

Archie lifted his head.

"She's fine, OK? We're going to rescue her. We're going to rescue all of them when we climb up that mountain."

Archie clenched his jaw. "I am going to rescue her."

"That's it!" Sir Hype said.

"I'm going to rescue her by doing something I should have done a long time ago. I'm getting out of here."

"Wait, wait, wait!"

Archie marched toward Ike. "I'm ready for that phone number."

"Awesome," Ike said. "It's 704 . . ."

"Don't do this," Sir Hype said to Archie. "Hey, we've got fireworks on the peak. You like fireworks, right?"

"... 555 ..."

Sir Hype turned his attention to Ike. "You remember how long we spent on this section? And you're just going to throw it away?"

"... 10—"

"AH!" Sir Hype yelled over the last two digits of the phone number.

Ike shot Sir Hype the same look parents give kids who are too old to be throwing a temper tantrum, then repeated himself. "... 10—"

"AHHHHHH!"

"You're gonna have to write it down anyway," Archie said. "I can't remember that whole thing."

Ike reached into his pocket, then furrowed his brow. He checked his other pocket. Then he glared at Sir Hype. "Where is it?"

"Where's what?"

"My pen! Where is it?"

"You think I took your pen?"

"Tell me where my pen is right now, or I'll tell everyone what's really going on."

"Wait, what's really going on?" Archie asked.

Sir Hype smirked. "Do you think that even one person will believe you over me?"

"What's really going on?" Archie repeated.

Someone near the front of the line screamed.

Sir Hype's smirk got smirkier. "Gordo." Then he cupped his hands in front of his mouth. "Don't worry! He's friendly!"

Several years ago, Sir Hype made friends with a gorilla named Gordo at an exotic zoo he'd bought for one of his videos. Although Sir Hype eventually lost the zoo due to a series of minor scandals, Gordo still served as a sort of mascot for his channel.

The version of Gordo guarding the pass up ahead had grown quite a bit since the last time Archie had seen him. On Earth, Gordo was a normal-sized gorilla—big enough to eat a person, certainly, but not much more than that. This video game Gordo could also polish off that person's family, pets, and home, while saving room to eat their minivan for dessert.

"Doesn't look friendly," Devil Doug said.

"He's friendly if you give him Hype Fuel."

"Where are we supposed to get Hype Fuel?!" Naila asked.

"At one of 3,700 retail locations worldwide, or get 20 percent off online by using the promo code 'MOUNTAIN

CHALLENGE FIVE.'" Sir Hype smiled at an invisible camera for a beat before saying, "You also have one other choice."

Sir Hype held his finger to his lips, then led everyone into a small cave off to the side of the path. Inside the cave was the same dragon that'd carried the Hype Squad away during the announcement video. He slept with his tail curled around several yellow barrels all labeled "HYPE FUEL."

"Here's how this works," Sir Hype whispered. "We have to sneak past the dragon and get those barrels one by one. If we can do that without waking the dragon, nobody dies. This isn't a race. Follow my lead, OK?"

"Not OK," Ike said a little too loudly.

"Shhh!" Everyone shushed Ike.

"Archie and I have something to tell you," Ike continued at the exact same volume.

Poomf.

Sir Hype threw Ike's pen into a clump of snow deep inside the cave.

Ike clenched his jaw. "So you did have it this whole time."

Sir Hype gestured toward the pen. "And now it's yours."

Ike looked like he wanted to say something, but kept his mouth closed and started working his way toward the pen, zig-zagging and hopping across the cave.

"He's walking like that because there are lots of cleverly disguised buttons on the ground," Sir Hype explained to the group. He pointed to a pair of giant speakers on the cave's ceiling. "One wrong move, and those go off. Then, it's a very different type of challenge."

"Why does he want the pen so bad?!" Naila asked. Then she turned to Archie. "What did he want to tell us?"

All the attention shifted to Archie.

"You had something to say?" Sir Hype asked Archie. "Go ahead. Now's your chance."

Suddenly, Archie felt hot. "Oh, um, so I didn't . . ."

AWOOOOOGA!

Oh no. The speakers!

AWOOOOOGA!

The dragon's eyes snapped open.

AWOOOOOGA!

"I didn't do anything!" Ike yelled. He started hoofing it back to the group.

AWOOOOOGA!

The dragon raised to its full height.

AWOOOOOGA!

Ike threw his tablet toward the group as hard as he could. Then, he yelled, "RUN!"

That was his last word before being swallowed whole.

CHAPTER FOURTEEN

LAW OF COOL

"This way!" Sir Hype sprinted back toward Gordo. Everyone followed Sir Hype except for two people. One was Naila, who'd scooped up Ike's tablet. The other was a brave, stupid soul who decided to become a legend by fighting the dragon alone.

"I DANCE WITH DANGERRRRRR!"

Unfortunately, that would be poor Benny's final dance. The dragon swallowed him in one gulp.

Sir Hype directed everyone to press their backs against the mountain. "All eyes on me," he said.

Hisssssss.

That was pretty hard to do with a giant dragon stalking out of the cave.

"ROOOOAAAAAAR!"

It became impossible when Gordo spotted the dragon. The gorilla beat his chest and bounded toward his nemesis.

The coffee mug decided it'd seen enough—it sprinted for the open mountain pass. Without breaking stride, Gordo scooped up the mug with his long arms and fired it at the dragon like a missile. The mug stuck in the dragon's left nostril. This upset the dragon quite a bit. It dislodged the mug by breathing fire, which sent the mug flying off the mountain like a firework.

"All eyes on me!" Sir Hype repeated.

Everyone obeyed this time.

Sir Hype rubbed his hands together. "Waking the dragon changed this from a stealth mission to a survival mission. I know my way up this mountain. The path may seem impossible at times, but you've got to trust me. Do you trust me?"

Everyone nodded.

"Follow me to survive."

The dragon and gorilla continued slugging it out in front of the cave. The dragon wrapped up Gordo with its tail, then the gorilla landed a massive right hook.

"Now!" Sir Hype sprinted toward the pass. Archie tried staying by his side but got pushed to the back of the line. Just before he entered the pass, he turned and made eye contact with Gordo.

"Grrrr."

Gordo pointed to the group while holding the dragon's head in the snow. At that moment, both beasts decided they had a new enemy.

"They're coming!" Archie yelled.

Up ahead, Sir Hype directed everyone to a row of snowmobiles. Archie grabbed the last one.

With no clear trail up the mountain, Archie was forced to forge his own path by weaving through trees spaced just far enough apart to fit a snowmobile. Since this was his first time on a snowmobile, that was a task easier said than done. Complicating things a bit further was the pesky dragon constantly trying to destroy him with fire.

Contestants started going down fast. Both Ronnie and Rhodie crashed into pine trees. Then, a puffy marshmallow got appropriately roasted. The dragon picked off an astronaut, farmer, and someone who appeared to be a fan of the 1980s cult classic sitcom *Alf*. But the dragon wasn't content with that. It had its eyes set on Sir Hype himself. The dragon swooped lower and breathed deep. Before the dragon could roast Sir Hype, Gordo roared from down below.

"ROOOOAAAAR!"

The gorilla's roar was so loud the dragon paused its attack. So loud that the air vibrated. So loud that the ground began to rumble. It took Archie a second to realize what'd just happened, but a pang of fear stabbed his heart once he did. Gordo had just triggered an avalanche.

When Archie saw the growing wave of snow and rocks cascading down the mountain, he hit the brakes. Several people turned around. Even the dragon had the good sense to fly away. The only person acting like nothing was wrong was Sir Hype. He sped faster than ever toward the avalanche.

Sir Hype's plan came together at the last possible second. Just before the avalanche swallowed him whole, it knocked over a tree in front of his snowmobile. That tree happened to split in the perfect place for Sir Hype to ride it like a ramp. He zoomed up in the air and hung for a moment above the avalanche. As glorious as that was, it would all be over in a moment when he fell back to Earth and got buried under a thousand tons of snow, right? Nope. Just before Sir Hype landed, another tree surfaced on top of the avalanche, providing him with another ramp.

The odds of that happening in the real world are worse than the odds of getting struck by lightning while scratching off the winning lottery number with a four-leaf clover. But this was a video game. Video games, you see, operate by the Law of Cool. The Law of Cool states that other pesky laws involving logic, gravity, and probability do not apply as long as the stunt is cool enough. And no stunt could ever be cooler than surfing up an avalanche.

Sir Hype continued using fallen trees as ramps to climb the mountain. One by one, the rest of the group followed. Archie gulped and gunned his engine. No turning back now. The avalanche built on itself, swallowing trees, tossing boulders, and shaking the earth. Then, a moment before it covered Archie, a tree ramp appeared.

Vroooooom!

Even though Archie had just watched Sir Hype make the jump, he had to close his eyes. He hung in the air for what felt like minutes then—*WHAM*—landed on another tree. He gunned the engine again.

Vroooooom!

"Wahoooooo!" Archie allowed himself a cheer as he flew again. The next time, he kept his eyes open. For the third jump, he pushed things a little too far and let go of the handlebars for a brief moment. That almost caused him to fall off the snowmobile when he landed. Over and over, the Law of Cool kept Archie safe as he sped up the mountain. On the final jump, he glanced back just in time to see the avalanche swallow poor Gordo.

POOMF!

Since Archie wasn't looking where he was going, he took the plunge into the snowbank hard. He stumbled to his feet and started limping toward the group. Sir Hype was leading them to a frozen lake. Suddenly, a shadow fell over the mountain. The dragon had returned.

WHOOOSH!

The dragon blasted the frozen lake with its fire, melting ice and causing geysers of steam to shoot into the air. The dragon found this so delightful that it swooped back around and spit twenty more fireballs across the lake before circling to the other side of the mountain. The lake was now divided into hundreds of tiny icebergs.

"This way!" Sir Hype sprinted toward the ice. Devil Doug, a safari explorer, and an elf princess followed right behind him. Jin-Soo, Naila, and a group of kids were next. Then, there was Archie, hobbling at the back of the line.

When Sir Hype jumped from the first iceberg to the second, his momentum carried the iceberg too far for everyone else to make the same jump. "That one!" He pointed to a nearby iceberg.

Devil Doug and the explorer attempted the jump at the same time. Thanks to a vicious midair shove, Devil Doug landed on the iceberg alone. He raised his fist to celebrate a victory that would last for exactly two seconds.

CHOMP!

A prehistoric whale with teeth leaped from the water and swallowed him whole.

"Not that one!" Sir Hype pointed to another iceberg. "That one!"

The princess dove for the other iceberg. The whale got her too.

"You wanna figure this out?!" Naila yelled at Sir Hype.

"Just follow my lead," he replied.

"That didn't work out so well for those guys!" Naila shot back.

"Trust me!"

With no choice but to trust, Naila and Jin-Soo led the kids across the frozen lake by following Sir Hype's path. Archie followed, too, just a little slower due to the limp.

Finally, Sir Hype reached a cave on the other side of the frozen lake. Next came Naila and several small children. Jin-Soo brought up the rear.

"Hurry!" Sir Hype called to Archie.

Archie was trying to hurry, but he couldn't remember which iceberg came next.

"That one!" Sir Hype pointed to the ice on Archie's left.

"No, the other one!" Naila yelled.

A shadow fell over the mountain. Archie didn't need to look up to know that meant the dragon had returned. He followed Sir Hype's direction.

Immediately, the prehistoric whale returned. It leaped out of the water with its mouth wide, ready to swallow Archie whole. At the same time, the dragon swooped in. It also had its mouth open wide, ready to roast Archie whole. Up close, both beasts looked scarier than Archie remembered. The whale had an evil glint in its eye and the dragon wore yellow slime on its face. The only suspense left came from trying to guess which monster would get Archie first.

The answer, surprisingly, was neither. That's because the game chose this exact moment for its first glitch.

CHAPTER FIFTEEN

THE STORYTELLER

For a brief moment, the whale and dragon both turned pixelated like they were buffering. Then, they froze in place. That gave Archie the opening he needed to scramble onto the next iceberg and dive into the cave. As soon as he did, a door shut behind him and lights flickered on.

"Was that a glitch?!" Archie asked.

Sir Hype ignored the question because he was too busy celebrating. He clenched his fists, looked to the ceiling and screamed, "Let's gooooooo!" as if he'd just scored the winning goal of the World Cup.

"Because if that was a glitch, then we're in big trouble," Archie continued.

"Nice job, nice job, nice job." Sir Hype worked his way down the row of kids, giving out high fives so aggressive that they looked like they hurt. He lit up when he reached Naila and saw that she still had the tablet. "Oh, nice! You rescued that."

"Mm-hmm," Naila replied, tapping on the screen.

Sir Hype reached for the tablet, but Naila yanked it away. He gave an amused smile. "That doesn't have any games on it. It's not a toy."

"I'm figuring out if it'll get us out of here," Naila replied.

"That's just a monitor for watching video," Sir Hype replied. "You can't make any changes on it."

"Yeah, that's what I'm seeing."

Sir Hype reached again, but Naila spun away. This time, Sir Hype didn't smile. "What's up?"

Naila flipped the tablet around. She'd pulled up a video from just a few minutes before. There was Ike, creeping toward his pen in the cave. There was the group surrounding Archie. And there was Sir Hype, off to the side. Naila pressed "play."

"You had something to say?" Sir Hype asked Archie in the video. "Go ahead. Now's your chance."

While everyone watched Archie stammer and stutter, Sir Hype crept toward the cave. He located a small lump in the ground, then squashed it with his foot.

AWOOOOOGA!

So Ike hadn't set off the siren—it was Sir Hype! Naila paused the video and glared at Sir Hype. Time for him to squirm.

Sir Hype did not squirm. "You're welcome," he replied coolly.

"Excuse me?"

"You're about to be a star. So, you're welcome for that."

"I'm about to be dead," Naila replied. "We're all about to be dead."

"Do you think I would let that happen?" Sir Hype asked.

"Before every challenge, you say no one is going to die, and then a bunch of people die! So, yeah, I think it's going to happen. Pretty soon, there won't be anyone left to climb the mountain, and there's not a single thing you can do about it."

"I think I can help you feel better. You wanna know what's really going on?" Sir Hype reached for the tablet, but Naila yanked it away again. "Fine," Sir Hype said. "Rewind back to the first challenge. The one with the falling platforms."

While Naila did that, Sir Hype smiled at the group. "Have I told you guys my secret to becoming famous on YouTube? Hook, story, and payoff. That's it. The game is really that simple. But that doesn't make it easy."

Naila pressed "play." There was Sir Hype, explaining to the (much larger) group at the beginning of the platform challenge how they could ensure nobody would die. In the present time, Sir Hype continued his lecture. "Anyone can come up with a good hook. In this case, we lucked into the best hook of all time: climb the mountain or die."

"You're right, dying is super lucky," Naila said.

Sir Hype ignored her. "The hard part is the story. Stories need conflict. They need danger. They need heroes and villains, comedy and tragedy. You never get all that in real life. You might luck into a great hook, but you never luck into a great story. If you want a great story, you need to write it yourself."

Sir Hype nodded at the screen. All the contestants were following Sir Hype's count during the platform challenge. One-two-step. One-two-step. The camera zoomed in on Sir Hype. He smiled as he called out the timing. Then, he stuck out his left leg, tripping the coffee mug.

The kids all gasped. "Is that supposed to make us feel better?" Naila finally asked.

"Of course, it is." Sir Hype looked downright pleased with himself. "Here's what's really going on: you've never been in any danger. Everything that's happened today has happened because I wanted it to. You're in the greatest story anyone has ever seen. And I'm the storyteller."

Archie felt sick as he thought back on the past several hours. Sir Hype had manipulated him into continuing the game. He'd tricked him into saying "let's a-go" before anyone was ready for the second challenge. Sir Hype had been the one encouraging him to freeze his own cousin.

Naila shook her head. "I'm here because I'm good. I earned this."

"A bunch of people were good. Big Time Bryce was good. Devil Doug was good. Look around. What do you have in common?"

One glance around the cavern revealed that no one besides Sir Hype was older than thirteen.

"Eighty percent of all my video views come from children. A good storyteller knows his audience. I'm just giving them what they want."

Naila rolled her eyes. "Great. You're putting a bunch of kids in danger to grow your audience. Congratulations. You get even more money."

"I don't care about money."

"Now, I know you're lying," Naila said. "If you didn't care about money, you wouldn't live in that mansion."

"The mansion is a prop," Sir Hype replied. "I don't even live there. I spend most nights in the studio because all I want—all I've ever wanted—is to be the world's biggest YouTuber. I want to tell the world's biggest stories on the world's biggest stage. That's it. And guess what? This is what it takes. I'm reaching the top, and you're all coming with me."

"Not all of us," Naila said. "In the real Mountain Challenge, only one person reaches the top. If we're still following your script, that means only one of us gets to be the hero. So who is it?"

Archie shifted nervously. Sir Hype had promised that he'd be the one to summit the mountain. Was Sir Hype going to reveal his master plan to everyone?

"It's me," Jin-Soo spoke up. "I'm the hero. You said it at the beginning—the kid who can't walk climbs to the top of the mountain. What a story."

Sir Hype pointed at Jin-Soo. "There's the payoff," he said without a hint of shame in his voice. "As a bonus, you'll bring in lots of viewers since Asia is a growing market for my brand."

Archie's face turned red with rage. He wasn't mad at Sir Hype for taking advantage of Jin-Soo—no, he was upset

because he'd been played. Sir Hype had no intention of making him the hero. In fact, he'd actually just tried to kill Archie by directing him to the wrong iceberg.

Jin-Soo was also furious. "I'm not playing this game anymore," he said. "Find another hero." With that, he flipped open the guard on his wristband.

Sir Hype smirked and shook his head. "Buddy, you're not really going to abandon everyone, are you? They need you."

Jin-Soo locked eyes with Naila. "You got this?"

She gritted her teeth and nodded.

Jin-Soo pressed the button.

"No!" Sir Hype screamed with wild eyes. "Take it off! Take it off!"

Jin-Soo waved goodbye, then turned all blue and wavy.

"NO!" Sir Hype dove for Jin-Soo's wristband, then turned blue and wavy himself as soon as he touched Jin-Soo. The pair froze in place, screaming and glitching.

Then, they both disappeared.

CHAPTER SIXTEEN

THE HACKER

"All eyes on me," Naila commanded.

All eyes swiveled back to Naila. All eyes except for Archie's. He continued staring at the spot where Sir Hype had disappeared.

"Hey!" Naila clapped a couple times to get Archie's attention. "Don't worry about that guy. We didn't need him anyway."

One of the younger kids—a boy with big eyes and messy hair who appeared to be no older than six—started whimpering. Naila got down on his level. "Hey, bud. Sir Hype wasn't your friend. Did you know that?"

The kid shrugged and whimpered again.

"We need friends to get to the top. And guess what? We're all friends here. She's your friend. He's your friend. I'm your friend."

A little snort escaped Archie's nose. Naila looked up. Her eyes switched from compassion to absolute fury. "What was that?"

Archie deeply regretted that snort. "No, it's just—remember at the beginning when you said you weren't here to make friends?"

Naila glared harder if that were even possible. "I think I made myself pretty clear. I'm here to survive. And right now, the only way we survive is by working together. No more backstabbing. No more secrets." She looked around the group. "Anyone here plan on betraying the rest of us?"

Nobody moved—especially not Archie. He'd already betrayed the group but admitting that now wouldn't help anyone. Without that phone number, it'd be pointless for him to return to the real world. By the time he'd manage to reach Ike's team, months would pass inside the video game. Better to keep his mouth shut and try to make it up to the group by reaching the top of the mountain.

"Seriously," Naila said. "If you're in this for yourself, you'd better start moving now before I shove you off this mountain."

Absolute silence.

Naila turned to Archie with a sarcastic smile. "There you have it. Guess we're friends now."

To ease the tension in the cavern, a boy wearing a backward Charlotte Hornets cap made the unfortunate decision to start everyone's favorite cheer. "Hyyyyyyyyyy—"

"Not now!" Naila snapped.

The boy immediately stopped. Naila huffed, then led the way to a narrow opening in the back of the cave. The farther she walked, the darker it got, so she used Ike's tablet as a flashlight. The opening led to a swinging rope bridge suspended over a bottomless pit inside the mountain. The little boy started whimpering again, so Naila held his hand. The group barely breathed as they walked across the bridge.

"HYYYYYYYYPE!"

Archie jumped as the yell bounced off the cavern walls.

"NOT NOW!" Naila yelled before realizing the scream hadn't come from the group—it'd come from the tablet. Although she thought she'd switched on the flashlight earlier, she'd actually played a video. "Sorry," Naila mumbled as she fiddled with the screen.

"I dance with danger!" Benny shouted from the tablet speakers.

"Hang on, I think I need to . . ."

"WAHOO! WAHOO! WAHOO!" the tablet continued. Somehow, Naila had only managed to turn up the volume.

"What do you think about figuring this out on the other side of the bridge?" Archie asked.

Naila let the video play while she crossed the bridge, which meant the group had to relive the audio of that poor girl with the unicorn headband push the button on her wristband. Finally, after what felt like an hour, the group reached the other side.

The ground over here clanked like metal, but it was difficult to see much else without any light. Naila paused the video and started fiddling with the tablet's controls. "I thought I saw a flashlight somewhere over here."

"Get outta here, cup!" Naila's voice called over the tablet's cheap speakers.

"People call me 'K-Bear.'"

"I hate kids."

The greatest hits from the past few hours played as Naila tapped all over the screen to find the flashlight. Then, a familiar voice echoed through the darkness.

"I'M THE HACKER!"

Naila stopped tapping. Archie stopped breathing. After a moment, Naila tapped again.

"I'M THE HACKER!" Archie's voice repeated from the tablet.

More silence. Finally, Naila whispered in the darkness, "What does that mean?"

Archie cleared his throat. "So, I can explain."

Naila marched toward Archie and grabbed his shirt. "We're here because of you?!"

"No!"

Naila pressed "play" again. "I'm really sorry," Archie said in the video. "This is all my fault."

"OK, but I didn't do it on purpose!" Archie protested.

"If you got us in here, you can get us out, right?" Naila asked.

"No!" Archie replied, then changed his answer when he remembered the next part of the video. "I mean, I could have gotten us out before, but not now."

Archie could barely see Naila in the dim light, but he could feel her shaking with rage. "You could have rescued us?" she asked. "You could have rescued your own cousin? But you didn't?"

Archie opened his mouth for an explanation, but no words would come. Instead, a heaving sob escaped his throat.

"Get outta here," Naila said.

"I want to help," Archie begged.

"Go."

"I can help. Please."

Naila pushed Archie back. "OUT!"

"No. Please. Don't make me. Don't make me go."

Click.

Click.

Click-click-click.

As soon as Archie said the word "go," a series of floodlights clicked on, illuminating the next challenge.

The metal ground turned out to be a giant gear. That gear powered another gear, which powered a set of spinning blades, which guarded an elaborate pulley system, which tripped either a drawbridge or a set of crossbows. All that was on the first level of the challenge. One glance upward revealed at least twenty more levels of danger after that first one.

Crrreeeeeeeaaaaak.

The gear started turning.

CHAPTER SEVENTEEN

LOTS OF LEGOS

A hologram timer floated above the kids' heads. Twenty minutes remaining.

"Ahhhhhh!" The smallest kids held each other and screamed.

Naila tried calming everyone. "Here's what we're going tooo doooooo." Naila blinked a few times in confusion. She tried again. "No matter what, we stick tooooooooog-g-g-g . . ." Naila's expression changed from confusion to panic. Why couldn't she finish her words? "Together-er-er-er."

Archie suddenly found it hard to breathe. His lungs started working in slow motion, which caused him to try taking deeper breaths. When that didn't work, he joined Naila in panic.

Tink.

A screw hit the ground near Archie's feet.

Tink, tink.

Next came two bolts.

CRASH!

That was followed by the face of a giant clock.

Archie looked up to see parts raining down in slow motion. He pushed the Hornets cap kid away from a falling piston, then dodged a cannonball himself. He only needed a moment to figure out what was going on.

Too many Legos.

Thanks to the memory leak, all this intricate machinery had become too much for the software to handle. The game was slowing. Parts were breaking. The mountain had begun its collapse.

Archie sprinted toward the spinning saw blades in slow motion, then dove for safety. He wouldn't normally find comfort in whirling blades, but for now, they provided a small awning of safety as he plotted his next move. The rest of the group quickly joined him.

"IIIIII thiiiiiiiiiiink weeeeeeee . . ." Archie tried talking strategy with Naila, but she wasn't interested. Instead, she rolled through the blades and tugged on a rope. A drawbridge lowered.

"Leeeeeeettttt's goooooooooo!" Naila yelled. Everyone ran for the bridge.

Whoooooosh-whoooooosh-whoooooosh-whoooooosh.

A flaming helicopter propeller fell toward the draw bridge. Agonizing seconds ticked by as kids crossed one by one ahead of impact.

Finally, only one contestant remained: Archie. He felt like he was fighting an ocean made of mud as he pushed his body to move faster. He looked up at the propeller. He wasn't going to make it. In one final desperate move, he dove across the bridge.

CRASH!

The flaming propeller sliced the bridge in two. As the bridge gave way, Archie scrambled to the other side and clawed onto the edge of the platform. The bridge fell into the abyss, while Archie tried pulling himself up.

"Heeeeeeeeeeeeeelp!" he yelled.

Naila walked to the edge of the platform and peered over. Archie held out his hand for help. Naila walked away.

"HEEEEEEEEEEEEELP!"

CRUNCH!

Something huge hit the platform, shaking Archie loose.

"Ahhhhhhhhhhh!"

As Archie tumbled down the pit, he watched the platform above crumble, dumping all the kids.

Everyone was dead.

CHAPTER EIGHTEEN

THE TOP

As Archie fell farther into the abyss, he started feeling fuzzy. Images scrambled in his brain—Mae rambling about her latest craft turned into Devil Doug trying to ram him with his Nissan Altima turned into Naila walking away from that ledge. The falling eventually stopped, and the swirl of images melted into one. The world was so dim that Archie needed a minute to figure out what he was looking at, but he finally realized that he stood in the back of a badly damaged school bus.

When Archie tried taking a step, he found that his legs didn't work—at least, not how they were supposed to. His legs couldn't carry him down the aisle because an invisible force was pressing his chest against the back door. Archie fought against the force and kicked his legs. He still wasn't getting anywhere.

"You're lying on your back," a voice called.

Archie froze.

Sir Hype poked his head into the aisle. "Took me a minute to figure it out myself."

Seeing Sir Hype's head helped Archie reorient himself. The bus wasn't on its wheels like normal; instead, it was pointing straight up like a rocket ship. When Archie realized the force on his chest was just gravity, he sat up, then climbed rows of seats like rungs of a ladder until he reached the row across from Sir Hype. He plopped down on the back of the seat and stared at Sir Hype. "Where are we?"

"A bus."

"No kidding. Where's the bus? Where's everyone else? Where's Jin-Soo?"

Sir Hype shrugged.

"What does that mean?!"

"I don't know, man. It's a bus. What you want from me?"

"I want to get out of here."

"Yeah." Sir Hype's voice sounded hollow.

Archie fell silent. For a minute, everything was quiet except for a faint rubbing sound. "What is that?" Archie finally asked.

"If you rub your fingers together, the skin comes off in, like, little blocks," Sir Hype replied. "I think they're pixels."

"Then maybe don't do that."

Sir Hype continued rubbing.

Archie sat still for another minute before saying what was on his mind. "I trusted you."

Sir Hype stopped rubbing. "You want my autograph?"

"Excuse me?"

"I never gave you my autograph, did I? Why don't I do that for you? I could autograph your shirt. Do you have a marker?"

"What . . . How . . ." Archie sputtered before he could finally finish his sentence. "Why would I want your autograph?!"

Sir Hype shrugged. "I thought it'd make things better."

"You wanna make things better?! Maybe start with an apology."

That got a little chuckle out of Sir Hype.

"You think that's funny?!"

"No, it's just—I told you. That's not me."

"Yeah. I'm learning a lot about who you are."

Sir Hype went silent and started rubbing his fingers again. Finally, he mumbled, "I've had time to reflect on my actions, and I am deeply sorry for the harm I have caused. In the days ahead, I hope to . . ."

"What are you doing?" Archie interrupted.

"Apologizing."

"That's not a real apology."

"Yes, it is."

"That's a YouTube apology!"

"I don't know what that means."

"Can you just be a real person for one second?!" Archie exploded.

More finger rubbing.

"Dude!" Archie yelled.

"Um, so, here's something I learned," Sir Hype said. "You can get anything in life if you want it bad enough."

This comment had absolutely nothing to do with the conversation at hand, but Archie let Sir Hype go because he was too exhausted to keep arguing.

"Whatever you want," Sir Hype continued. "Fame. Money. Power. You can have it as long as you want it so bad that you'll do whatever it takes to get there."

"Sounds easy," Archie said sarcastically.

"Feels easy while you're doing it. It's like, every decision is so simple, ya know? What do I need to do right now—this minute—to get to the top? How do I climb that mountain? You do that day after day, year after year, and then you finally get to the top, and it's like . . ." Sir Hype spread his hands.

"What?" Archie asked.

"I dunno. You're at the top. You're by yourself. That's it."

Archie squinted, a little confused. "OK."

"I'm someone who climbs mountains, all right? I've only wanted one thing for so long that this is who I am now. Sorry if that's not what you were looking for, Peyton."

"Archie."

"Huh?"

"You called me 'Peyton.' My name's Archie."

"Oh." Sir Hype sniffed. "I knew it was one of the Mannings."

Archie didn't understand the reference, and he certainly didn't understand the man in front of him. "But you're a real person. You're Roy."

"Mm-kay."

Archie tried opening the window to his right. When that didn't work, he climbed up to the next row and tried opening that window too. "Why don't you help get us out of here?" Archie asked.

Sir Hype squished deeper into his seat. "We're not getting out."

Archie rattled another window. "Appreciate the optimism."

"This is where people like me go when they die."

"Really?" Archie asked. "You think this is, like, a bus of eternal torture or something?"

At that moment, a song started faintly playing. Archie recognized this song as a tune so catchy, and yet so annoying, that he had to consider Sir Hype's point. Maybe they were being tortured.

"Ba-doo-bee-doo, my baaaaabyyyy!"

"Told you," Sir Hype said.

Archie gritted his teeth and started climbing toward the music. The driver's window of the bus was open, allowing Archie to squirm out. That squirm out the window turned out to be just the beginning of Archie's squirming. The bus was buried beneath a mountain of motorcycles and pizza costumes and cracked sewage pipes and a whole landfill worth of junk. Archie fought off claustrophobia as he squirmed up through garbage toward the music. That terrible music. Light started filtering through from up above. Finally . . .

"MY BAAAAAAAABYYYYY—"

Click.

Archie turned off the music, collapsed in the seat of the mangled Kia Rio, and stared at the sky. He'd made it.

"Hey!" someone squealed. "Turn that back on!"

Archie froze when he heard the voice. Could it really be her?

"I said to turn that back on!" Mae crawled onto the hood of the car.

CHAPTER NINETEEN

JUNK MOUNTAIN

"AAAAAAARRRRRRCH!" Mae squealed when she saw her cousin's face. She dove into the car and wrapped Archie in a hug.

"Mae!" was all Archie could say before she squeezed his neck so tight he couldn't talk.

"You're safe!" Mae continued. "I was worrieder than worried for you!"

Archie squirmed out of Mae's death grip and looked her in the eye. "Mae, I'm sorry. I'm so sorry I did all this to you."

Mae went right back to squeezing Archie's neck. "It's OK, Arch!"

Archie squirmed out again. "No, Mae. It's not OK. I—I've done so many things." Tears filled Archie's eyes as words tumbled faster out of his mouth. "I could have gotten us out of here earlier—should have gotten us out of here earlier. I should never have used that ice sword on you. I shoulda—shoulda—Mae, I never even made your YouTube channel. We recorded all those videos, and I did nothing with them. If we ever get out of here, I promise . . ."

Mae interrupted Archie by squeezing his neck one more time. "We're gonna help people now, OK?"

Archie sniffed and nodded. After another few seconds, Mae let go, then cranked the radio full blast again.

"MY BAAAAAAAABYYYYYY!"

"THIS IS THE BEST WAY TO RESCUE PEOPLE!" Mae shouted over the singing. "THEY CRAWL UP TO SHUT OFF THE SONG!"

Archie blinked a few times. It finally occurred to him that he had absolutely no idea what was going on. He led Mae out of the car so he wouldn't have to yell. "Mae, where are we?" he finally asked.

Mae spread her arms. "Junk Mountain!"

Archie looked around. Mounds of junk towered in every direction, and none of it was in garbage bags. It looked like someone had destroyed a whole city, shaken everything together, then dumped it all here. The wreckage appeared to go on forever, although it was hard to tell for sure because of the snowstorm. The snow here was weird. The flakes were perfect cubes, almost like pixels. The strange pixel flakes swirled and whipped around, stinging Archie's face every time they touched his skin.

"Jacket?" Mae offered Archie an oversized zip-up hoodie from the trash pile with the words "Boy Mom" stitched on the front.

Archie took the garbage jacket and pulled the hood tight over his head. "So this is where people go when they . . ."

"Yuppers," Mae said. "This is where you go when you kick the bucket. It's a little scary at first, but then you find allllll this neat stuff. See?!" She picked up a cracked Muppets-branded popcorn bucket lying near her feet. "We've been rescuing people ever since I got here."

"Who's 'we'?" Archie asked.

"Yooooooo!" a voice called. "Got one!"

"Nice job, Yannis!" Mae yelled back.

"Yooooooo!" the same voice called from behind. "Me too!"

"Nice job, other Yannis!" Mae yelled again.

"Yoooooo!"

"Yoooooo!"

"Yoooooo!"

"Way to go, Yannises!" Mae squealed. When she saw how lost Archie was, she explained, "Remember Robot Yannis in the house at the beginning? Since everyone got their own, there are five hundred of them, and they're super helpful!"

"Yoooooo!" a dozen Yannises harmonized at once.

"This is the memory leak," Archie said to himself.

"The what?" Mae asked.

"The memory leak," Archie repeated, a little more excited. "This is what Ike was talking about, remember? Instead of deleting things when it's done with them, the game has been storing them here! Do you know what that means?!"

Mae still looked lost, but she bounced on her toes to match her cousin's energy.

"It means that there's still hope! It means we can still get out!"

"Weehee!" Mae squealed.

"Where's Ike?" Archie asked.

"Have we found Ike yet?" Mae called out to the Yannises.

"No, yo!"

"Then, let's get to work!"

Archie, Mae, and hundreds of Yannises got to work turning on every working car radio. Both fortunately and very unfortunately, every radio was programmed to play the same song on repeat.

"MY BAAAAAAAABYYYYYY!"

People began surfacing left and right to turn off the awful tune. There was Big Time Bryce and K-Bear. Jin-Soo and Devil Doug. The coffee mug made it to the surface—stained and rumpled, but still smiling as big as ever. Sir Hype finally broke out of his funk long enough to climb out of the bus.

As soon as people climbed to the surface, Mae would recruit them to her rescue operation. They'd help turn on radios, then get to work digging. While a good number of contestants could climb to the surface themselves, most had to be dug out by hand.

As Archie dug, small pieces of his skin would occasionally crumble off in cubes like Sir Hype's had done in the bus. He pulled his sleeves over his hands and tried not to think about it as he continued to dig. Finally, a hand emerged from the garbage. Archie took the hand and pulled.

It was Naila. "Thank . . ." she stopped herself when she saw who her rescuer was.

Archie nodded a quick acknowledgment and turned to continue his search.

"Hey," Naila said. "I should have pulled you up."

"I deserved to fall," Archie said.

"You did. But I still should have pulled you up."

"Thanks," Archie replied. "I think I have a second chance to get us out of here, but I need Ike. Can you help me find him?"

Naila pulled out the tablet, which now had a very cracked screen. "Check this out." She tapped a button, and a list of names filled the screen. "This gives you a live view of everyone in the game right now." Naila scrolled down to Ike, then tapped on his name.

"Help!" Ike cried as he pounded on something metal. "Helllllp!"

"Where is he?" Archie asked.

Naila rotated the camera until it focused on a thick, green tube next to Ike's head. "Fire hose!" Naila gasped.

"We're looking for a fire truck!" Archie shouted to the group.

"Yooooo!" one of the Yannises pointed to the top of a white ladder.

Everyone got to digging. It was tough work—the fire truck was buried under some brutally heavy equipment—but with everyone's help, Naila and Archie eventually pried open the fire hose compartment.

"WAHOOOOOOO!" everyone cheered Ike's least favorite cheer as he stumbled out.

"I'm ready for the phone number!" Archie told Ike. "Give it to me, and I'll get us out of here."

Ike squinted at everyone staring at him. Then, he looked up at the swirling snow. He caught a flake and rubbed it between his fingers. He shook his head. "It's too late."

CHAPTER TWENTY

MR. WHOOSH-WHOOSH

"It's not too late!" Archie said. "Everyone's still alive."

"See this?" Ike showed Archie one of the flakes. "This isn't a snowflake falling from the sky; it's a pixel rising from the ground. This is what data corruption looks like. We've got seconds of real time and—I don't know—maybe an hour—in the video game before the hot spots come."

"But . . . but . . ." Archie sputtered.

"It's over. We're dead." Ike had remained remarkably matter-of-fact while sharing this terrible news, but his voice quivered just a bit during the next sentence. "Just—um—just make sure you tell our story when you leave."

"Leave?" Big Time Bryce asked. "Why does he get to leave?"

"Oh! Uh, he doesn't get to leave." Ike realized a little too late that he was about to start a riot. "What I meant was . . ."

"I'm the hacker," Archie interrupted. The group went silent. Archie took a deep breath. "That means I'm the reason you're here. That means you can blame me for everything bad that's happened. And, for some reason, that means I get to go home while the rest of you have to die in a dump."

Archie stared at the ground while he spoke so he wouldn't have to see the angry mob. He was tempted to glance at Mae for support, but he didn't think he could handle the disappointment in her eyes.

"I'm sorry," Archie said. "Obviously, it's too late for that, but I need you to know I'm sorry. I wish I could go back in time and undo everything, but for now, I'm going to take this off and give it to someone who deserves it." Archie removed his wristband and handed it to Mae.

"Oh, pretty!" Mae said. "But I already have one."

"This one works," Archie said. "It'll take you home."

Mae's face lit up. "We can go home?!"

"You can go home."

"You need to come too."

"I can't. That's not the way this works."

"Then, I don't want to go." Mae handed the wristband to Naila.

Naila shook her head and passed it onto the little girl wearing the unicorn headband. That girl immediately passed it onto a boy dressed as a dog next to her, who passed it onto the coffee mug next to him. The mug looked back and forth, then strapped the band around its wrist.

"NO!" everyone yelled at once, in firm agreement that someone should go back to the real world, but under no circumstances could it be this ridiculous coffee mug. The mug quickly unstrapped the wristband and handed it to Sir Hype.

Sir Hype stared at the wristband for a long moment. "Do it!" a voice shouted from the crowd.

"You deserve it!" said someone else who'd clearly not gotten caught up on all of Sir Hype's misdeeds.

"Hyyyyyyyyype!" people started to cheer.

Sir Hype held up his hand to stop the cheering. "You all think you know me because of who I am in front of the camera. You don't know me. Today, some of you saw the real me. Maybe for the first time, I saw the real me. The person I saw was selfish. He was ugly. That person is why you're here today, but that is not the person I want to be. I'm sorry."

"Never apologize!" yelled a dude wearing a suit with torn-off sleeves.

"What's your name?" Sir Hype asked.

The man puffed out his chest a little. "Diesel."

"Hey, Diesel? I don't care about your name. I'm going to forget it in one second. I'm just using it to make you feel special so you do what I want."

Diesel deflated.

"See?" Sir Hype asked. "Selfish. Ugly. I've been this way for a long time, and it's hurt a lot of people." He turned to Ike. "I'm sorry." Then, he looked back at Diesel. "Sorry, Diesel."

"All good, man."

"I'm sorry, Archie."

Archie nodded.

Sir Hype walked the wristband over to Jin-Soo. "I'm so sorry for the way I used you. I hope you can forgive me one day."

Jin-Soo hugged Sir Hype. He then took the wristband and handed it over to Yannis.

"Dope!" Yannis said. Then, he passed the wristband on to one of the Robot Yannises.

"Dope!"

For the next five minutes, the wristband passed from Yannis to Yannis.

"Dope!"

"Dope!"

"Dope!"

"Dope!"

Finally, the last Yannis passed the wristband on to Devil Doug.

"Haha!" Devil Doug cackled as he strapped the band onto his wrist. "See ya, suckers!" Then, he mashed the button.

"NOOOOO!" everyone screamed.

Nothing happened.

Devil Doug pressed the button again. Still nothing. He wiggled the wristband and tapped again.

"Yeah, that's not going to work," Ike said.

"What?!" Devil Doug exploded.

"Obviously, Archie's the only one who can use the wristband," Ike said. "If someone else could have used it, I would have taken it a long time ago."

"Then, why did you let us pass it around for the last ten minutes?!" Naila asked.

"It was a really nice moment!" Ike replied. "Probably won't have many more of those before the end."

Whoosh. Whoosh.

Just then, the snow got extra swirly as something whooshed above.

"Oooooh, Mr. Whoosh-Whoosh is back!" Mae pulled a bottle of mustard out of her pocket.

"Who's Mr. Whoosh-Whoosh?" Archie asked.

Whooooooooosh.

The dragon swooped through the snow and dive-bombed toward the group. While most people dove for cover, Mae threw her mustard. She missed the dragon miserably, but hit K-Bear right in the tummy, squirting mustard all over her costume.

"Eeeeeek!" K-Bear appeared absolutely horrified that her last few minutes on Earth would be spent in a stained costume.

Suddenly, Archie remembered something. "Mae, have you thrown one of those before?"

"Yes! Last time he was here. I thought Mr. Whoosh-Whoosh learned his lesson."

Perfect. There just might be one more way off this mountain.

CHAPTER TWENTY-ONE

I WAS WRONG

"We're on the back of the mountain," Archie told Ike.

"No way," Ike replied. "Not possible."

"Yes!" Archie insisted. "The last time I saw the dragon, he had yellow slime on his nose. Or, at least I thought it was yellow slime. But now, I know it was mustard!"

Ike looked lost.

"Mae threw mustard at the dragon earlier," Archie explained. "I saw the mustard right after he'd finished circling the mountain. That's gotta mean that Junk Mountain is just the backside of the real mountain!"

"But there's no reason for junk to accumulate back here," Ike said.

"The memory leak!"

"That's not how memory leaks work!"

"What's going on?" Sir Hype interrupted.

Ike shook his head. "He's saying that the memory leak is junk on the back of the mountain, but that's not something that could have happened by itself. I would have had to program that into the game on purpose."

Sir Hype gulped.

Ike squinted at him. "Did you do that on purpose?"

"You know how I like to fool around with the code."

"Dude, what?!"

"I just moved a couple things back here while I was trying some stuff! How was I supposed to know that it'd do all this?! You should have told me . . ." Sir Hype trailed off when he saw the look on Ike's face. "No. You're right. It's on me. I'm sorry."

"But isn't this good news?" Archie asked. "Because if we're on the same mountain, then we can still climb to the top!"

"Maybe," Ike said. "But now, we don't just need one person to make it. Because of the data corruption, everyone who wants to live has to reach the portal."

"What happens if someone doesn't make it?"

Ike shook his head. "That's it. No second chances."

This news pumped new life into Sir Hype. "Hyyyyyyyyype!" he yelled. In an instant, he transformed right back into a YouTube star. He climbed on top of the nearest vehicle—a food truck named Rocco's Macho Tacos— and yelled, "The video's back on!"

Everyone turned toward Sir Hype.

"We can still escape if we reach the top of this mountain. It's not going to be easy. Every single person here will need to work as one. We'll have to—Hey! Where are you going?" Sir Hype stopped in the middle of his speech to call out Naila, who was starting to hike by herself.

"We're seriously doing this again?" Naila asked. "Greatest video ever made? Big speech? Rah-rah? And you actually think people are gonna fall for it a second time?"

The crowd started murmuring.

"I'm serious this time," Sir Hype said. "We've gotta stick together if we want to survive."

"Good luck on the video," Naila replied coldly before turning around.

"I was wrong!" Sir Hype blurted.

Naila stopped walking.

"I was wrong," Sir Hype repeated. Then he looked at the sky and yelled, "I WAS WRONG!" one more time for good measure before turning to Ike. "Did that work?"

Ike shook his head and pointed at Archie. "He has to be the one to do it."

Archie was totally lost. "Do what?"

"When we programmed voice commands, I told him to pick one that stops recording," Ike explained. "Since he never wanted to stop recording, he picked the one phrase he knew he'd never, ever say: 'I was wrong.' But since you're the Game Master, you're the only one who can do the voice commands."

"Can you say it?" Sir Hype asked Archie. "Please. Only one thing's important right now, and it's not the video."

Archie nodded. "I was wrong."

"There," Sir Hype said. Then, he called out to Naila, "Are you with us?"

Naila looked down at the tablet, saw the recording had ended, and took a deep breath. "Let's climb."

CHAPTER TWENTY-TWO

HOT SPOT

The group began their long trek up the mountain with Sir Hype leading the way and a gaggle of Robot Yannises bringing up the rear. At first, the climb was easy. Sir Hype called out a cadence that everyone marched along to. "Hype-two-three-four! Hype-two-three-four!"

But soon, the climb grew steeper. The death snow swirled harder. People started slipping. Then, the group arrived at their first big obstacle—a five-story hotel planted right in their path. Walls of junk and rock prevented them from hiking around the hotel, and a blockade of smashed mini fridges in the lobby kept them from going through it. The only way past the hotel was over it.

"We got this, yo," the real Yannis said. Then, he called to all his robot brethren. "Stack 'em up!"

The Robot Yannises responded with a chorus of "yo's" and got to work. The first group lined up across the hotel on their hands and knees, then the second group climbed on top of them and did the same thing. The Yannises stacked on top of each other until they formed the world's tallest human pyramid. When the final Yannis capped off the pyramid inches from the hotel's roof, the group cheered.

One by one, everyone climbed the tower of Robot Yannises. Sir Hype was the last one up. When he reached the roof, he got down on his belly and held out his hand to help up the top Yannis.

Robot Yannis shook his head. "We can't all make it up."

"But you can," Sir Hype replied.

Robot Yannis smiled. He had the tiniest tear in his eye. "Yannises stick together. Together, we rise, and together we faaaaaaaaaa . . ."

That's when the Yannis tower collapsed. All five hundred Robot Yannises tumbled into a pile.

"Yo!" The real Yannis stood on the hotel roof, holding up his fist in salute.

The Robot Yannises all hopped to their feet and returned the salute.

"Yooooooooooo!"

What a nice moment. Even nicer was the fact that the path up the mountain picked right back up from the hotel's roof. Then, something not-so-nice happened: a huge, furry hand shot up through the garbage. A second hand emerged. Those hands swiped away trash, clearing the way for a King Kong–sized gorilla head.

"ROOOOOOAAAAAR!"

Gordo looked horrible. His fur held on to his skin only in patches. The whole left side of his face looked pixelated.

Benny pushed to the front of the group, so he was face-to-face with Gordo. "I've got this!" he yelled to the group. Then, he pounded his chest. "Wanna dance? LET'S DANCE!"

Gordo lifted himself fully out of the trash, balled up his fist, and smashed.

Benny dove away. Then, he screamed one word in Gordo's face.

"I!"

Gordo swatted. Benny hurdled over the gorilla's arm.

"DANCE!"

Gordo lunged. Benny rolled.

"WITH!"

Gordo finally scooped Benny in his big mitt and held him up to his face. Benny was not deterred.

"DAAAAANGERRRRR!"

Gordo growled and opened his mouth wide for a snack. Then, his eyes shifted to the ground. He immediately dropped Benny.

"That's it," Jin-Soo said. "Little closer, bud." Jin-Soo had found a barrel of the one substance on Earth that could tame the giant beast: Hype Fuel. Jin-Soo waved the barrel back and forth as he slowly backpedaled to the edge of the mountain. "You want it? Go get it!" He wound up to heave the barrel over the mountain.

"DON'T!" Sir Hype yelled.

That stopped both Gordo and Jin-Soo.

"Give it to him," Sir Hype said.

"But he . . ."

"Trust me," Sir Hype interrupted.

Jin-Soo considered that for a moment before lifting the barrel over his head. Gordo immediately shoved the whole thing into his mouth. Suddenly, the gorilla's eyes turned bright green. He stood to his full height, beat his chest a few times, and let out a mighty roar. Then, he grabbed Jin-Soo.

"You just made a friend for life," Sir Hype yelled. "Hang on!"

Gordo placed Jin-Soo on his back and started galloping. The rest of the group tried to keep up as Gordo blazed a

trail up the mountain. Thanks to the amazing power and significant sugar content of Hype Fuel, Gordo tossed aside heavy machinery, punched through brick walls, and stomped obstacles flat. Gordo made record time up the mountain until he reached the one obstacle he couldn't muscle his way past: a snowstorm.

It'd been snowing all the way up the mountain, but this storm was something else entirely. While the previous cubed flakes of death had been blowing and swirling, these streamed straight into the sky. The snow was much thicker here, too, producing a wall of white that hid the rest of the mountain.

After taking a moment to size up the storm, Gordo peeked back at Jin-Soo to get his take.

"Let's do it," Jin-Soo said.

Gordo beat his chest, then sprinted forward.

"NO!" Ike yelled when he saw what was happening.

"AAAAAHHHHHH!" Jin-Soo started screaming from inside the storm.

"ARRRRRGGGHH!" Gordo screamed along.

"Get them out!" Ike yelled.

Archie reached into the storm, then pulled back immediately. It felt like he'd just stuck his hand into a bonfire. He tried to shake his arm and flex his fingers, but couldn't. Mae attempted to follow her cousin's example, but Archie yanked her away just in time. "What is that?!" Archie asked.

"Hot spot!" Ike tried the same thing as Archie with the same result. Meanwhile, the screaming coming from inside the storm grew louder and more distorted.

Archie shook Ike. "What do we—"

BOOF!

Just then, Jin-Soo hurtled out of the hot spot like a missile and slammed into Archie.

"Are you OK?!" Archie asked.

Jin-Soo struggled to stand and collapsed. "We've gotta—" he heaved a couple breaths that sounded like they were being played through a digitizer. "We've gotta help Gordo."

The noises coming from inside the hot spot no longer sounded apelike. Instead, they sounded like the awful screeches of a dying arcade machine.

"There's nothing we can do," Ike said.

Unable to walk, Jin-Soo tried crawling toward the hot spot. "He got me out. Now, it's my turn to help."

Ike held him. "Everything in there will be destroyed in seconds. He's probably gone by now."

The noise faded almost immediately after Ike finished his sentence. After that, the hot spot dissipated too.

"Whoooaaaa," Archie whispered.

With the snow gone, it became clear that the hot spot had claimed Gordo along with everything else it'd touched. It looked like someone had used the world's biggest ice cream scoop to carve a perfectly smooth crater into the mountain. But the crater wasn't what had earned Archie's "whoa." Balancing on what was left of the mountain just beyond the crater stood the mountain's peak. Atop that peak was a glowing, purple portal, surrounded by boxes of fireworks.

For one second—one glorious second—Archie had hope. Then, the mountain's peak collapsed into the crater.

CHAPTER TWENTY-THREE

KABOOM

"No!" Ike yelled. He led the way up to the collapsed peak and moaned. "No, no, no, no!"

The portal was gone now, buried in the crater under tons of digital rock.

Sir Hype wasn't ready to give up hope just yet. "Dig!" he commanded.

Unfortunately, digging up here wasn't like digging at the junk site. Every rock felt like it weighed a million pounds. Even with everyone working together, the group couldn't make a dent. One by one, people gave up. Finally, Sir Hype laid down in exhaustion.

"So, like, what do we do?" K-Bear asked.

Sir Hype didn't respond.

"The payoff," she prodded. "Hook, story, payoff. This is the payoff part. So what do we do?"

"No payoff," Sir Hype said. "Not today."

Devil Doug stood over Sir Hype. "I'm not leaving without a payoff."

"You're not leaving period." Sir Hype sat up. "This is it. Congratulations, you made it to the top. Why don't you enjoy the view before you die?"

As if to punctuate his point, another hot spot appeared toward the bottom of the mountain. The group watched in silence as it wiped out more garbage.

"You know what I would enjoy?" Devil Doug finally asked. "Tossing you over this mountain. That'll be my payoff."

"Yeah!" a tough-guy voice shouted from the crowd.

Devil Doug took a menacing step closer to Sir Hype.

"Not now, man," Sir Hype said.

"No, I think now is actually the perfect time." Devil Doug grabbed Sir Hype's legs. "Who's with me?"

Most people covered their mouths in horror, but a few stepped up to help Devil Doug.

"Cut it out," a shaky voice said. Jin-Soo had finally arrived at the peak. He had his arm around Naila, who'd helped him up the mountain.

"You want a piece of him first?" Devil Doug asked. "I'll hold him down for you."

"No."

"You realize he did this to you, right? You don't have to take it anymore."

"I'm not taking anything," Jin-Soo replied.

"Hey, don't worry. No one will see—we stopped recording." Devil Doug was doing his very best impression of the devil on Jin-Soo's shoulder right now. "Why not work out some of that frustration?"

"Why not?" Jin-Soo asked. "Why not?" He looked around at the group like he was gearing up for a big speech. Instead, he broke down into a ten-second coughing fit. When he finally recovered, he delivered the one-sentence version of his speech instead. "That's not the person I choose to be."

For a few seconds, the only sound on the mountain was Jin-Soo continuing to cough. Then, people backed away from Sir Hype. Devil Doug rolled his eyes.

The person I choose to be. Those words stabbed at Archie. He had a choice, didn't he? Even now—even at the end. He squeezed his cousin. "Hey, I'm going to do something that's, um, that might be dangerous."

Mae's eyes lit up. "You're going to rescue everyone?!"

"No. I mean, probably not. I think it's too late for that. But there's something I wanna try."

"Can I try too?"

Archie shook his head. "I've gotta do this by myself. And I think it means I won't get to be with you for the end."

Mae hugged her cousin tighter. Archie hugged back with tears streaming down his face. "Stay with Naila, OK?"

"I love you, Arch."

"Love you too, Mae."

When Mae reluctantly let go, Archie found Ike. "Hey," he said, holding up his wristband. "This is a bomb, right?"

"A what?!" Ike asked. "Definitely not."

"But that's what Robot Yannis said at the beginning!" Archie insisted. "He said it's a little bomb that blows you into a million pieces when you press the button."

"I mean—OK, fine—I guess that's technically true," Ike conceded. "But there are so many better ways to word that."

"Since my wristband is the only one that works, let me try to uncover the portal by blowing up these rocks."

"You don't want to do that," Ike said.

"Why not?"

"That explosion is almost certainly too small to do anything. You'll have wasted your only way out for no reason."

"I'm not leaving," Archie quickly replied.

"Fine. Let's say it's big enough to blow up the rocks. In that case, you'll have to run far away to stay safe from the debris. The countdown on the wristband is way too short for that."

"I know," Archie said. "I wanna try anyway."

Ike shook his head like he thought Archie was crazy. "Your choice." Then he shouted to the rest of the group. "Hey, gang! We're moving down the mountain!" He turned back to Archie with the tiniest of smiles. "Just in case."

When everyone finished moving a safe distance away on the non-garbage side of the mountain, Archie stood on the spot where he guessed the portal was and stared at his wristband. He took a deep breath. In Sir Hype's version of this story, the hero would be gritting his teeth and flexing his muscles, ready to save the day. In reality, Archie was seriously considering using the wristband to save himself now that no one else was up here to judge him.

The more Archie thought about his original plan, the worse he felt about it. If he would have stood there for five more seconds, he likely would have convinced himself to just use the wristband for his own escape. Instead, he flipped open the plastic shield, mashed the button, then tossed the wristband like a grenade.

KABOOOOOOM!

The wristband exploded even faster than Archie had been expecting. He tried running away, but the resulting shockwave knocked him to the ground. He covered his head to protect himself from the boulders falling all around him.

BOOM-BOOM-BOOM-BOOM!

That first explosion was followed by dozens more as Archie's blast set off all the fireworks Sir Hype had placed next to the portal for the winner. Archie tried crawling away, but a boulder landed on his leg. Another rock landed on his back.

"AHHHHHH!"

Even though searing pain pulsed through his whole body, Archie had to look back to find out if he was successful. He was rewarded with a purple glow.

"We did it!" he called. "We found the portal!"

BOOM-BOOM-BOOM-BOOM!

More explosions. Archie covered his head and listened for cheering down the mountain. Instead, he heard panic.

"Chestnut!" Sir Hype screamed.

Then, Ike's voice. "AVALANCHE!"

CHAPTER TWENTY-FOUR

SUPERHERO

Adrenaline gave Archie the strength to squirm out from under the rocks and peer over the edge of the mountain. The noise from his explosions had indeed set off an avalanche, but things were so much worse than that. Another hot spot had formed just below the group, and the avalanche was funneling everyone down there.

Archie tried standing up, but quickly collapsed back to the ground. He scanned the mountain for his cousin. "Mae!" He couldn't see anything down there except for snow—surging, deadly snow. "MAAAAAEEE!"

For a moment, nobody answered back. Then, Sir Hype repeated himself over the roar of the avalanche. "CHESTNUT!"

Suddenly, Archie understood. Sir Hype had only spoken that word twice—once just before he got crushed by a boulder during the snowball fight and right now. Maybe "chestnut" wasn't a family-friendly expletive after all. Maybe Sir Hype kept repeating it because he expected it to do something. Maybe "chestnut" was like "go" or "I was wrong"—a code word that only had power when spoken by the Game Master.

"Chestnut," Archie whispered.

Whooooooooosh.

Time immediately slowed to a crawl. The avalanche appeared to halt. Archie felt a jolt of energy. "Chestnut" turned out to be the most powerful code word in the game because it transformed the Game Master into a superhero.

Archie sprang to his feet and charged down the mountain. His pain had been replaced by Flash speed and Hulk strength. Inside the avalanche, Archie spotted Devil Doug frozen upside down, about to get crushed by a rock. Archie effortlessly pulled Devil Doug out of the avalanche, carried him up the mountain, and threw him into the portal. One down. The next person Archie rescued from the avalanche was Jin-Soo. Two down.

Back and forth Archie went—ten times, twenty times—so many times that he lost count.

Yannis. Big Time Bryce.

He started getting into a rhythm.

K-Bear. The mug.

Eventually, he figured out that he could rescue three people on each trip by piling them onto his back.

Ike. Ronnie. (Or was it Rhodie?) Rhodie. (Or maybe Robbie?)

Toward the bottom of the avalanche, he found a group of the smallest kids.

Unicorn headband girl. Charlotte Hornets hat boy Benny.

He rescued people until the entire avalanche was clear. Still, there was no sign of Mae. Only one place left for her to be. Archie gritted his teeth and charged into the hot spot.

"AHHHHHHHHHHHH!"

The superpower offered no protection from the hot spot. Archie's face felt like it was melting off. His mouth froze into a scream. Still, he pushed further into the hot spot. His vision turned to static. His hearing stopped working. Finally, he bumped into a body. Archie grabbed an arm, then ran back out of the hot spot.

He'd rescued Sir Hype.

Archie dropped Sir Hype off at the portal, then returned to the hot spot. This time, he hesitated for a second before running in.

"AHHHHHHHHHHHH!"

The pain was so bad that Archie couldn't stop himself from shaking. He pulled out another body. It was that Diesel guy. Archie continued shaking as he dropped off Diesel and returned to the hot spot.

Six times Archie returned to pull another person out of the hot spot, and six times he grew weaker. On the seventh time, he fell down as soon as he entered the hot spot. By now, he was shaking so badly that he couldn't stand back up. "MAAAAAAEEEEEE!" he screamed.

He pulled himself forward on his hands and knees one foot at a time. One inch at a time.

"MAAAAAAEEEEEE!"

Archie's finger brushed an arm. A very skinny arm. An arm so skinny that it could only belong to one person. Archie clutched the arm, stood up, then dragged one final body out of the hot spot.

It was Mae.

But not just Mae! Because wrapped tightly around Mae, doing everything in her power to protect the young girl, was Naila.

Archie dragged Mae and Naila out of the hot spot, through the avalanche, and up the mountain. Finally, just as his superpower started wearing off, he held on tight to both of them and tumbled into the portal.

CHAPTER TWENTY-FIVE

HYPELIGHTS

If Archie's journey into the video game had felt like a roller coaster with all its twists, turns, and hills, his trip back out of the game better resembled a ride through a paper shredder.

Crunch! Scrunch! Screeeee!

His body smooshed, stretched, and bumped around all the same turns he'd slipped through last time. Pressure built on every side as Archie felt like he was being squeezed into a tiny tube. Eventually—

Ptooooooooo!

Archie rocketed through darkness before finally landing in a heap. He groaned. Lots more people groaned around him. Someone screamed in the distance. Archie tried sitting up, but found that impossible to do, as he was buried under a tangle of bodies. The screaming continued while everyone tried to get their bearings. Finally, the screamer identified herself.

"Archie?! ARRRRRCHIIIIIIE!"

Archie's eyes widened. "Mom!" he yelled into someone's thigh. He pushed through the pile to find that every person on the mountain had ended up back in his house. "MOM!"

"WHERE DID ALL THESE PEOPLE COME FROM?!"

"Mom, where's Mae?!"

"Over here, Arch!"

Archie spun around to see Mae as the top of a Benny-Naila-Mae sandwich. Mae grinned at her cousin. "We're all here!"

• • •

"We're live?"

"Live."

"Three. Two. One. HYYYYYYYYYYYPE! What up hypeheads, this is Zac."

"And this is Xander."

"Together, we are HYPElights, your number one destination for Sir Hype news, rumors, and reacts."

Zac and Xander—two skinny guys who'd both made the tragic decision to mimic Sir Hype's beard despite their genetic inability to grow more than a few wisps of facial hair—grinned for the camera. These past few days since the mountain challenge website had mysteriously gone down had been the busiest days yet for their HYPElights channel. Speculation was swirling from every corner of YouTube, and Zac and Xander had planted themselves at the center of it all.

"So far, we've had lots of rumors and reacts, but no official news," Zac said.

"Not unless you count that hockey fan who said he'd already climbed the mountain," Xander pointed out.

"We are filing the Devil Doug video under 'rumors,'" Zac said. "But as of this moment, we are out of the rumor zone. Two minutes ago, Sir Hype posted a video with a shocking title. We have not watched it yet. You ready to react, Xander?"

Xander clicked "play" on a video titled "Apology." In the video, Sir Hype sat alone in his studio. His eyes looked all puffy like he hadn't slept in a few days, and his beard appeared scragglier than normal. He also wore a colorful bead necklace.

"Hyyyyyyy . . ." the HYPElights crew began in anticipation of Sir Hype's normal greeting.

"Hey, this is Roy," Sir Hype started. "I know you probably have a lot of questions for me. I have—uh—I have a lot of questions for me too. We'll get to the answers when the time's right, but for now, I just have one thing to say. I'm sorry."

Sir Hype took a deep, shaky breath, giving the HYPElights crew the perfect space to insert their reaction. Instead, they sat in stunned silence.

"I know this is the part where people usually say they've had time to reflect on their actions, but I haven't yet. Not really. I've been too busy talking to the people I've hurt. I just know that I'm sorry—really, really sorry—for the type of person I've chosen to become. This—um . . ."

Sir Hype looked nervous for this next part, but he forged ahead anyway.

"This is going to be my final Sir Hype video. I'm pulling the plug on my channel effective immediately. I know that's going to be hard for many of you to understand, but I think my decision will make more sense in the coming days as more of the truth comes out."

With that off his chest, Sir Hype looked like he could breathe again.

"I do have one final video coming," he said with a smile. "It's a collaboration with a wonderful young lady I've recently had a chance to meet. Why don't you check out her channel when you get a chance? It's called 'Arts and Crafts and Jewelry and Fun with Mae.'"

ABOUT THE AUTHOR

Dustin Brady writes books for kids who think they hate reading. His *Trapped in a Video Game* series has sold over two million copies because—as it turns out—there are a lot of kids who think they hate reading. Dustin loves *Tetris*, pinball, trick-shot videos, and many other silly pastimes that he calls "book research" even though they very much don't seem like book research. He lives in Cleveland, Ohio, with his wife, three kids, and a small dog named Nugget. Dustin honestly can't believe he gets to do this for a living.

ABOUT THE ILLUSTRATOR

Jesse Brady started drawing pictures of his favorite video game characters when he was six years old and hasn't stopped making art since. He even married an artist! Jesse and his wife April started VEC Workshop in 2021, where they create art and animation together. Jesse can easily beat his brother Dustin at *Super Smash Bros.*, but *Mega Man* and *Metroid* will always be his favorites.

Bentley Carmone's twelfth birthday party has been—without question—his worst. You see, video game aliens just kidnapped all his guests.

To save his buddies, Bentley must team up with Polly, a gas station mascot who thinks she's from the future. Armed with a blaster and laser sword, Polly would be the perfect partner for this job if she could ever stop invading miniature golf courses and picking fights with semitrucks. Can Bentley get through to his new friend before it's too late?

AVAILABLE NOW!

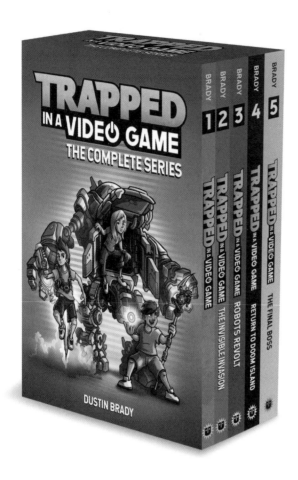

OVER TWO MILLION SOLD

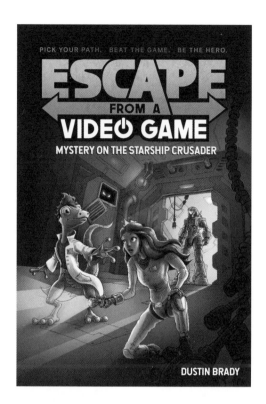

CONTROL THE ACTION